THE CASE OF THE
UNCONQUERED
SISTERS

THE CASE OF THE UNCONQUERED SISTERS

A HUGH RENNERT MYSTERY

TODD DOWNING

COACHWHIP PUBLICATIONS

Landisville, Pennsylvania

CONTENTS

Introduction, by Curtis Evans   7

1 Skull   13

2 Lead   15

3 Wire   20

4 Joke   21

5 Threat   26

6 South   35

7 Gun   45

8 Gold   52

9 Dusk   61

10 Drink   68

11 Fist   75

12 Clay   82

13 Loft   90

14 Shot   96

15 Owl   104

16 Yawn   110

17 Creak   116

18 Sleep   120

19 Blank   125

20 Pick   132

21 Key   142

22 Lie   149

23 Name   155

24 Proof   163

25 Hand   168

26 Hat   175

27 End   180

INTRODUCTION
CURTIS EVANS

"Mr. Downing is a born detective story writer."
—Edward Powys Mathers ("Torquemada"),
review of Todd Downing, *Vultures in the Sky* (1935)

THE RICHNESS AND DIVERSITY of American genre writing during the Golden Age of mystery fiction (c. 1920 to 1939) is much under-appreciated today. Golden Age mystery readers could choose from a wide variety of literary dishes, be it the tough stuff of the hard-boiled boys (most famously Dashiell Hammett, Raymond Chandler and James M. Cain), which has long received the lion's share of the attention that scholars have granted American Golden Age crime writers; the psychological suspense (or HIBK—Had I But Known—as it was once disparaged) of Elisabeth Sanxay Holding, Mary Roberts Rinehart, Mignon Eberhart and Leslie Ford; the urban sophistication of Rex Stout, Patrick Quentin and Rufus King; the madcap humor of Phoebe Atwood Taylor and Craig Rice (the latter making the tail end of the Golden Age); the eccentric extravaganzas of Harry Stephen Keeler; the police procedurals of Helen Reilly; the courtroom dramas of Erle Stanley Gardner; or the magnificent baroque puzzles of S. S. Van Dine, Ellery Queen, Anthony Abbot, John Dickson Carr, C. Daly King and Clyde B. Clason.

This listing of authors just scratches the surface of American mystery writing in the years between the two world wars. So many accomplished mystery writers from the period have undeservingly fallen into obscurity. One such individual is Todd Downing, the Golden Age chronicler of fictional murders in Mexico.

Todd Downing was born in 1902 in the town of Atoka, Choctaw Nation, Indian Territory (soon to be Oklahoma). Though one-eighth Choctaw and, like his father Samuel (Sam), an enrolled member of the Choctaw Nation, Todd Downing had what in many ways was a traditional, early twentieth century small town American upbringing. Both Todd's father Sam and his mother Maud were staunch churchgoing Presbyterians and Republicans and Todd was brought up according to the proper precepts of these two orthodoxies.

Yet the Downing family of Atoka was unusual in its great love of reading. From an early age Todd Downing could be found in nooks and corners of the family's two-story foursquare house with his nose buried in books. He particularly loved romantic tales of adventure, played out in settings around the globe. Beginning with Sir Walter Scott's and H. Rider Haggard's colorful sagas of derring-do, Todd moved on, in his teenage years, to crime and mystery, in the form of the short story collections of Arthur B. Reeve, creator of the virtuous scientific detective Dr. Craig Kennedy, and the novels of Sax Rohmer, creator of the diabolical criminal mastermind Dr. Fu Manchu.

After Todd became a student at the University of Oklahoma in 1920, he soon discovered Edgar Wallace, the awesomely prolific English king of the thriller. Todd devoured Wallace shockers at a prodigious rate. (His library of books, bequeathed at his death in 1974 to Southeastern Oklahoma State University, included sixty-five Wallace novels and short story collections, as well as Wallace's autobiography and biography.) Yet as the 1920s progressed, Todd, like many bright people in his day, became increasingly interested in fair play detective fiction, where the point is not emotional jolts but cerebration: the reader tries to solve the mystery for her/himself through clues provided within the text by the author. Over the decade of the twenties Todd purchased detective novels and short story collections by Anthony Berkeley, Earl Derr Biggers, Lynn Brock, G. K. Chesterton, Mignon Eberhart, Rufus King, Marie

Belloc Lowndes, Baroness Orczy, Mary Roberts Rinehart, T. S. Stribling and S. S. Van Dine.

Between mysteries Todd managed to find time to qualify for his B.A. and M.A at the University of Oklahoma, as well as to take classes in Spanish, French and anthropology during summers spent at the National University of Mexico. In 1928 OU hired the young Atokan as an instructor in Spanish. (Todd was fluent in five languages: English, Choctaw, Spanish, French and Italian.) In addition to teaching his OU classes and conducting summer tour groups in Mexico, Todd continued voraciously reading both detective novels and crime thrillers; and in 1930 he began reviewing mysteries of all sorts in the literary pages of Oklahoma City's *Daily Oklahoman*. Especial favorites of Todd's in the mystery line were Agatha Christie, Dorothy L. Sayers, Ellery Queen, John Dickson Carr, Dashiell Hammett, Mary Roberts Rinehart, Mignon Eberhart and additional worthy writers who likely are less familiar to many today: Anthony Abbot, Rufus King, H. C. Bailey, Eden Phillpotts and Anthony Wynne (for more on Todd Downing's mystery fiction reviews see my book *Clues and Corpses: The Detective Fiction and Mystery Criticism of Todd Downing*).

Encouraged by an older colleague at the University of Oklahoma, Professor Kenneth C. Kaufman, Todd Downing wrote his first detective novel in 1931, not long after he had begun contributing mystery fiction reviews to the *Daily Oklahoman*. Eventually published in 1933, *Murder on Tour* introduced Todd's most important series detective, United States Customs Service agent Hugh Rennert, who would appear in seven detective novels between 1933 and 1937. (A Hugh Rennert novella, probably written by Todd in 1932, was published in 1945.) Besides *Murder on Tour* these are: *The Cat Screams* (1934), *Vultures in the Sky* (1935), *Murder on the Tropic* (1935), *The Case of the Unconquered Sisters* (1936), *The Last Trumpet* (1937) and *Night over Mexico* (1937). All six of these later novels now have been reprinted by Coachwhip Publications.

The Hugh Rennert detective novels are primarily set in Mexico (the one exception being *The Last Trumpet*, where the action ranges from Cameron County, Texas to the Mexican state of Tamaulipas). Todd Downing's authoritative and fascinating use of Mexico as a setting in his detective novels makes him one of the most important regionalist mystery writers of the Golden Age and is his most significant contribution to the genre. Additionally, the Rennert novels are graced with teasing fair play puzzle plots, stylish writing and interesting characterizations. Hugh Rennert himself is a notable detective, modest, middle-aged, self-reflective and somewhat melancholy, yet resolute and determined. ("A good kind man," one character calls him in *Night over Mexico*, and he is.) Hugh Rennert is fascinated with Mexico and *vacilada*, the mirthfully stoic attitude of the country's people toward life and death; and over the course of the series Todd Downing explores what might be termed the metaphysical relationship of Rennert and Mexico in interesting ways. We learn a lot about both a man and a country.

After 1937 Todd Downing wrote two more detective novels, both with a different series detective (Texas sheriff Peter Bounty, introduced in *The Last Trumpet*): *Death under the Moonflower* (1938) and *The Lazy Lawrence Murders* (1941). He also published the work which he considered his crowning achievement as a writer, a non-fictional study of Mexico, *The Mexican Earth* (1940; reprinted by the University of Oklahoma Press in 1996). Sadly, Todd's attempt in the 1940s to write a mainstream historical novel about Mexico came to naught. Todd had resigned as an instructor at the University of Oklahoma in 1935 in order to devote himself professionally to writing, but after 1941 he would never publish another novel—indeed, after 1945 he never published any fiction of any kind again. In the 1940s Todd found employment as an advertising copy writer in Philadelphia. One of his ads, the tongue-in-cheek mystery homage "The Case of the Crumpled Letter," was chosen in 1959 as one of the 100 greatest advertisements.

In the 1950s Todd returned to the teaching profession, taking posts at schools in Maryland and Virginia, but after the death of his father in 1954 he returned to Atoka to live with his octogenarian mother and teach Spanish and French at Atoka High School, from where he had graduated thirty-five years earlier. After the death of Todd's mother in 1965, Todd lived on alone in the old family home until his own demise in 1974. The professional highlight of his later years was his appointment as Emeritus Professor of Choctaw Language and Choctaw Heritage at Southeastern Oklahoma State University (then Southeastern State College). Reflecting Todd's continued interest in his Choctaw heritage were his series of lessons in the Choctaw language, *Chahta Anampa: An Introduction to Choctaw Grammar*, and his historical pageant play about the Choctaw Nation, *Journey's End*, both of which were published in 1971, forty years after he penned his first detective novel.

Todd Downing is buried beneath a simple headstone in Atoka, the place of his birth. Fittingly, his writing lives after him.

1
SKULL

WHERE THE GROUND slopes sharply away from the Texas end of the International Bridge at Laredo, exposing the layers through which the Rio Grande has cut its bed, two men stood in the sun and gazed at a low hand truck on a railway siding.

The older, more deeply tanned man had both fists propped against his hips and was shaking his head discouragingly.

"What an unholy mess! What is it?"

"Bones," his companion answered, holding his eyes narrowed to a squint against the glare of the sun.

The other glanced at him and spat on the close-packed gravel.

"Keerist!" he ejaculated in mock amazement. "I wish I'd had a college education. Here I was thinking it was a croquet set."

"I mean," the younger man explained seriously, "it's a shipment of prehistoric skeletons going to a museum in the United States."

He averted his eyes to watch a group of naked Mexican children splashing in the shallow water below. He had only three months in the border customs service behind him and still felt resentful at the river for the way it had disillusioned him. Some damned fool in a cramped New York room had written a romantic lyric about a rose blooming by the Rio Grande. He had never seen this muddy stream trickling through sand to the gulf, that was certain. Roses, hell!

The older man had walked over to the truck and was poking a stick into the debris of desiccated bones and cracked plaster and the splintered wood of packing cases.

13

"Well, we never know when we're well off, do we, Crockett?" he commented. "I thought I had a lousy job, going through the grips and groceries of every Mex and tourist who crosses the line. But this *would* be a sweet way to spend your time—digging up these old boys. They got kinda busted up when that baggage car was derailed, didn't they?"

"Yes. Everything else is up at the customs house. I'm waiting for them to come for this."

"Where'd they dig up these bones?"

"Near Mexico City, I think." There had been a sharp note in the question, which made Crockett turn his head. "What's the matter?"

The other was leaning over the edge of the truck, his face blurred by the shimmering heat waves sent up by the rails.

"How long they supposed to 've been dead?" he asked.

"I don't know. Thousands of years, I suppose. Why?"

"Thousands of years, huh? Well, there's something rotten in Mexico then. This baby here ain't been dead no thousand years. Come take a look."

Crockett approached and glanced down at the skull, neck vertebrae and shoulder blades which a fracture in the gray-white plaster had laid bare.

When he turned away there was a suspicious whiteness about his lips. "Looks like you're right," he said weakly.

"I know damn well I'm right! See here, son, you run up and get Doc Drexel. And you might notify Rennert, too." The man laughed dryly. "Rennert likes murder cases."

"Murder?"

"Yeah. Take a squint at the bullet hole in this skull. You can't tell me they had bullets in Mexico a thousand years ago."

2
LEAD

"Busy, Mr. Rennert?"

The young man paused on the threshold of the bare boxlike office.

Hugh Rennert laid down his pen and settled back in the swivel chair, so that the breeze from the diminutive electric fan played over his thinning brown hair.

"Hello, Crockett," he said cheerfully. "I'm always busy at this time of year. But come in and tell me what's on your mind."

Crockett sat on the edge of a straight-backed chair.

"It's about the baggage car that was derailed this afternoon, Mr. Rennert. The railroad people cleared the track and loaded the damaged stuff onto hand trucks on the siding. I was there keeping an eye on things until they went through the customs. McCook came along and got to looking at the last truck. There was a shipment of skeletons on it, in plaster casts, going to a museum in the United States. They were pretty badly broken up. He called my attention to something and thought I ought to notify you."

"Yes?"

"Two of the skeletons were old and dried up. But one of them was recent. That is, the man hadn't been dead very long."

"It was in a plaster cast, too?"

"Yes, just like the rest. No one would have noticed the difference if the casts hadn't been broken. There was something else, Mr. Rennert. There's a bullet hole in the skull."

Rennert leaned forward. "You're sure of that?"

15

"Yes. I told Dr. Drexel, and he went down to look at it. He had the whole truckload taken up to his office. Was that all right?"

"Certainly. Is anyone accompanying this shipment of skeletons?"

"Yes. There was a young man with them in the baggage car after they went through the Mexican customs. He was knocked unconscious. Dr. Drexel has him in his office now."

"To whom was this shipment consigned?"

"The Teague Museum in San Antonio."

"Very good, Crockett. Thank you. I'll go over to the doctor's office at once. You might try to locate the fellow's luggage."

"Yes sir."

Lowering his hatbrim against the afternoon heat that stabbed at his eyeballs, Rennert set out across the bare expanse of sand to the frame building where Dr. Drexel presided over his antiseptics and vaccines.

He waited in the outer office while the youthful assistant penetrated into the inner sanctum. In a few moments Drexel came out, clad in the white apron that always made his tall, rawboned frame look as if it were in a strait jacket.

"Hullo, Hugh."

He sank into a chair, indulged in his usual witticism about the weather and went on without a pause:

"The M.D., having viewed the body, states that it is that of a male, age uncertain as yet, about five feet eight inches in height. Deceased has been in that category approximately six or seven weeks, part of the time reposing in lime. Cause of death probably this." He opened his left fist over a sheet of paper and let fall a pellet of lead. "It penetrated the middle of his forehead to the brain. Make what you can of it, Sherlock, and tell me—since when have jobs like this been a part of my duties?"

Rennert smiled. "Come, come, Doctor! I only wanted to find out whether you really were an M.D. or just took a course in needle jabbing."

He scrutinized the bullet for a moment, then replaced it on the table.

"What about the other skeletons?" he asked.

"I'd say that Gaul was still divided in three parts when they were put underground."

"They're that old?"

"Undoubtedly."

"Any clothing or other means of identification?"

"Nary a bit of clothing. No signet ring, no broken cuff link, no scrap of paper clutched in the bony talons. There's a dental plate that might help though."

"Good. I understand that you have here the young man who was hurt in the wreck. May I see him?"

"You may look at his youthful physiognomy, if you wish, provided you don't try to fingerprint him or give him the third degree yet. He's still unconscious from a rather nasty crack on the head. A fractured wrist, too, I think. I don't believe he's seriously hurt, but you can't tell about these head injuries. I've got him in the inner office. Want to go in?"

"Yes."

Drexel got up and led the way into a small adjoining room where sunlight filtered through drawn blinds.

On an iron cot against the far wall lay a man clad in underwear. A sheet covered the lower part of his body, and bandages swathed the right side of his head. Against so much whiteness his tanned face looked like a dark nut on whose compressed surface features had been carved. He had a square chin and well-shaped mouth, both emphasized by the lean line of his jaw, a short, blunt nose and a wide forehead marred by a scar over the left eyebrow. The outward tilt of the tips of his ears and the arc of lighter skin where the black, springy hair began to recede were the results, evidently, of wearing a hat a great part of the time.

He was of medium height and slender, but the bare left arm which lay upon the sheet was tightly muscled and the hand large and calloused.

As Drexel bent over to explore the bandages with long, delicate fingers, Rennert turned to the clothing draped upon a chair at the foot of the bed. There was a snap-brimmed straw hat stained by perspiration, a suit of tropical worsted and a pair of square-toed tan shoes.

Rennert felt in the inside pocket of the coat and brought out a billfold and two long manila envelopes. He carried them into the next room and sat down at Drexel's desk. Too many years in the customs service, he reflected, give one a sublime disregard for the privacy of another man's possessions.

One of the envelopes contained a passport dated the previous October and made out to John Clay Biggerstaff, of San Antonio, age twenty-six. The purpose of his sojourn in Mexico was given as archaeological work.

In the other envelope was a permit whereby the Teague Museum was authorized to export from Mexico three skeletons. These were described in some detail. They belonged to what was specified as the Archaic culture and had been discovered at San Angel, a suburb of Mexico City. Their age was estimated to be two thousand years. The lengthy and profusely stamped document had been signed by an inspector of the Department of Archaeology of the Mexican government.

The billfold of tooled Russian leather showed the marks of long usage but was obviously an expensive one. The name "John Biggerstaff" was stamped on one of the flaps. Rennert frowned suddenly and slanted it against the light. "John Biggers," he saw, was the name which had been put there originally. Later the "taff" had been added. To an unpracticed eye the difference in the lettering would not have been noticeable.

Rennert continued his examination. Inside he found ninety-odd pesos in Mexican bills and the return portion of a Mexico City–Laredo ticket. Between the two flaps, protected by a slip of glassine, was the photograph of a girl.

Her hair seemed to be blowing in the wind, and she was laughing as she held one hand to keep it in place. She wasn't an exceptionally beautiful girl, although her features were well molded in a small, oval face. Her eyes were dark and wide-spaced on either side of a high-bridged nose.

Across the bottom of the photo had been written "Love, Cornell."

Rennert looked up as Dr. Drexel came into the room. The latter caught sight of the object of Rennert's attention and came to stand at his shoulder.

"So this is how our overpaid customs men spend their time! Gazing at tokens of young love. Nice-looking girl, isn't she?"

"Yes," Rennert agreed abstractedly. His eyes traveled away from the laughter on the girl's lips to the thing which lay like a bruised dead bug on the white paper.

"Ugly, isn't it?" Dr. Drexel's voice softened. "The girl, the boy and—that. It'd be easy enough, Hugh, to pass the buck on this. Ship the body on through and let the museum in San Antonio worry about it."

"I know," Rennert said. "Don't tempt me."

Drexel laughed dryly as he watched Rennert's eyes go to the window which framed the Rio Grande and, beyond it, the flat deserts of Mexico melting into a haze of heat.

"Hell, Hugh, you can't fool me. You're straining on the leash already, scenting clues. You're as bad as the Mikado for taking your crime seriously. Well, I'll go take another look at our Mr. X."

He went out whistling,

"*My object all sublime,*
    I shall achieve in time,
  To let the punishment fit the crime,
    The punishment fit the crime."

3
WIRE

HUGH RENNERT
UNITED STATES CUSTOMS
LAREDO, TEXAS

DENTAL PLATE BELONGED PROFESSOR
GARNETT VOICE ON LEAVE FROM SOUTHWEST-
ERN UNIVERSITY FOR RESEARCH IN MEXICO
STOP OTHER DESCRIPTIONS CORRESPOND
STOP IDENTIFICATION SURE STOP WIRE INFOR-
MATION
JAMES KERRIGAN
CHIEF OF POLICE

4
JOKE

THERE IS A WINDOW of the United States Embassy in Mexico City which looks out over lush green grass to cream-colored walls draped with masses of crimson and magenta bougainvillaea.

In the middle of a June afternoon a worried man sat at a desk by this window and took his eyes unwillingly from contemplation of the quiet sunlit scene. He was an extremely important man in various spheres of activity in two countries. Most Mexican newspapers and those American ones of a certain political leaning accoladed this importance by referring to him as a personage.

He looked now in the open appraisal which is the privilege of the mighty at the man who sat across from him.

This man sat erect, yet at ease, and smoked with evident and unassumed pleasure one of the cigars from the box of lacquered wood on the desk. The Personage liked his quiet air of competence, the cut of his features—homely and at the same time distinguished—the firm, square chin offsetting a hint of sensitiveness about the lips. Most of all he liked the clear, direct gaze of the brown gray-flecked eyes.

"Mr. Rennert—" he spoke with ponderous precision—"there have been many confidential conversations in this room. In the course of them I have asked many men for assistance in official matters. A few, a very few, I have asked for personal favors. This time my request is both official and unofficial."

On the rostrum he had acquired the knack of clearing his throat so as to graduate the emphasis which he wished to place on his next words. Now there was an impressive and prolonged vibration of the cords in the fleshy throat.

"I suppose it is no secret to you that I am responsible for your journey to Mexico City. It is my duty, of course, to look into the death of a citizen of the United States, particularly when it occurs under suspicious circumstances. There is no doubt about the identification of this body, is there?"

"None at all."

"Of course. I knew you must have made sure before you took any steps. Now, I could have gone ahead with an investigation with the assistance of our own staff, the Mexican government and the federal district police. This is the procedure which would be followed in ordinary circumstances. I am going to explain to you why I wished someone not connected with any of these groups to take charge. I am going to be quite frank with you, Mr. Rennert, since I rely on your discretion. When I have finished, I want you to express yourself just as frankly. If you do not care to become further involved in the matter, simply say so. I assure you that I shall have no criticism to make of your decision. Is that understood?"

"Perfectly." Rennert's smile was pleasant—and noncommittal.

"Very well then." Here began a groping for words which did not escape Rennert's attention, despite the increase of diplomatic gravity which was intended to hide it. "You may or may not know how much political influence the Teague interests have in the Southwest" (It seemed for an instant that there was going to be a pause here, but there wasn't), "where my constituency is. I hope for obvious reasons that we can avoid antagonizing them. I have no theory at all to advance as to how the body of this professor came to be found among the archaeological specimens consigned to the Teague Museum. Perhaps Mr. Roark, to whom I am going to introduce you in a moment, will have. What I wanted to impress upon you is the need for extreme delicacy in handling this situation."

Through the heavy silence drifted the hum of traffic on the street outside the walls. Rennert had leaned forward to knock the ash from his cigar and returned to the same position. He made a good listener, the personage thought. He didn't try to show interest by interposing interjections or betray impatience by fidgeting. (To tell the truth, Rennert was mildly amused by this preamble. He remembered rumors that occupancy of this important foreign office was a step on the road to the United States Senate. He knew how much smoother Teague oil could make that road.)

The dignified voice went on, a little more easily:

"The embassy has a particular interest in this affair for another reason. Mr. Voice appealed to us this spring for protection. He was worried on account of some letters."

"Letters?" Rennert said a bit sharply.

"Yes. He had been receiving letters, supposedly from some Mexican bandit, threatening him with abduction and bodily harm unless he paid a sum of money. He came here in a state of considerate agitation. He showed me one of the letters."

The speaker turned a pair of steel-gray eyes on Rennert's face. "I wonder if you have any idea how common such occurrences are, Mr. Rennert? How often United States citizens come to the embassy with such stories?"

"Frequently I imagine."

"Almost every month. Sometimes it is merely an excuse to enter and look around the embassy. Sometimes it is a desire for publicity. More often it's nothing but a practical joke that has been played on some simple-minded tourist by his friends. So many of them come down here with the idea that Mexico is overrun with outlaws. If there isn't a bandit scare they are disappointed. There was one instance where a group of Americans actually hired some Mexicans to kidnap one of their friends and hold him for a day or two out in the mountains. You have no idea how much worry this causes us. We can't treat the matter lightly to their faces or they will write indignant letters to newspapers in the United States. It's very difficult to know what to do."

Another throaty sound.

"When Professor Voice came to me with this letter I didn't take it very seriously. He seemed just the type of man to be made the butt of a joke. He had a wild story about owls gathering about his window at night. He was so obviously terrified, however, that I sent one of the young men on our staff, Mr. Roark, out to San Angel with him. He was living with the Faudree family there. Roark was to question Voice more fully, examine the letters and then, if he thought there was any basis for apprehension, call in the Mexican police."

"Do you recall the date of Mr. Voice's visit?"

"It was toward the end of April. Mr. Roark will be able to tell you more definitely. He reported that in his opinion Voice was really afraid but that the whole thing was a practical joke."

"Did he specify on whose part?"

A moment of hesitation. "One or both of the young men in the Teague party, he thought. They haven't been out of college long. We didn't hear from Voice again, so dropped the matter. Now it seems we were too hasty. Your mission will be to make up for our negligence, in a way. It will be complicated by one more consideration. Are you acquainted with the name of the Faudrees?"

Rennert nodded. "I believe the family has been established here since the Civil War."

"Yes. One of the families of Southern irreconcilables who took up Mexican citizenship. There are two sisters and a niece left. Unfortunately both Voice, who was a distant relative, I believe, and the Teague party were staying at their home, so that your investigation will have it as a starting point. Now the Faudree name still has some prestige here. These women, of course, are not concerned in this matter, and I hope you won't find it necessary to worry them. I have been informed confidentially that you are acceptable to the Mexican authorities, Mr. Rennert, and that they will delay taking any action until you make a report. Now, that's the job. Do you want to undertake it?"

Rennert's eyes met the steel-gray ones without wavering.

"You realize," he said quietly, "that it is not impossible that I shall have to pick a murderer from one of these two groups. The Teague party or the Faudree family. You asked me to speak frankly. Can I rely on your support—regardless of what I discover to be the truth?"

The other got up and walked slowly to the window, where he stood with his head half turned away, staring out at the bougain-villaea.

"You aren't taking the bandit idea seriously then?" he asked.

Rennert was blunt. "Are you?"

The personage emitted a low sigh, and a look of weariness crossed his face as he turned back into the room.

"No, Mr. Rennert," he said heavily, "I'm not." He paused. "I know that I have seemed to put expediency above the primary consideration that a crime has been committed. I assure you, however, that I want to see justice done. Whatever you discover, whatever action you see fit to take, I will back you up."

"Very well," Rennert said. "I'll take the case."

"Thank God, Rennert!" It was a spontaneous outburst. "I don't have words to express my gratitude. You can name your compensation." He took an envelope from a wire basket and handed it to Rennert. "Here is a letter which I had Roark draw up. I have signed it. It will serve as a credential for you in case you have need of it."

His hand sought a button on the edge of the desk.

"I'm going to turn you over to Mr. Roark now. He is at your orders as long as you require him. Roark is a very good man. He was educated in the United States. A brilliant scholastic record. He has lived a great part of his life in Mexico and speaks Spanish fluently. He has a future ahead of him, I believe, if he remains in the service."

There was a long-drawn-out pause.

The personage said companionably, "Have another cigar, Mr. Rennert."

5
THREAT

AT FIRST GLANCE Delaney Roark seemed to conform to the type of foreign service man with whom Rennert had come in contact so often. He was tall, well-built but without the carriage of the athlete, and his gray suit had the cut of an excellent and expensive tailor. He had a long, thin, boldly handsome face, with a high forehead from which his sleek blond hair was brushed sharply back. There was an air of restrained nervous tension about him, and his gray-blue eyes looked tired, with slightly discolored pouches beneath them.

He took Rennert's hand with just the right amount of warmth, listened with polite lack of attention to something in the nature of a homily from the personage behind the desk, then escorted the visitor to a smaller office down the hall. There he soon had him ensconced in a chair which, while it was not as comfortable as the one which he had left, was more conducive to relaxation.

He seemed sincere in his desire to put Rennert at his ease and to stamp their relationship at the outset with informality. He held out a creased package of a popular make of cigarettes, grinned at the sight of Rennert's cigar, then rested his coattails against the edge of the desk by an uncovered typewriter.

"Well, that's over with," he said as he flicked a match in the general direction of an ash tray. His voice was soft and pleasant, with the labial effect of a man who speaks a Latin tongue a great deal. His full, rather sensuous lips held the cigarette tilted upward. "The old man is inclined to be long-winded sometimes."

"It *did* take him quite a while to tell me that I was going to have to depend on you for my information."

"He's worried, all right. Worried as hell. I haven't seen him like this in months. You seem to have given a good poke at a hornet's nest."

"It looks like it. I only hope this letter you were kind enough to draw up will afford me some diplomatic immunity from their bites."

Roark's eyes took on a bit of life. There was a speculative quality to them. "I see what you mean. That you're liable to be the fall guy. It's happened before. But you don't need to worry about that in this case. The old man wants to keep his political waters well smoothed with Teague oil, but he's a square enough shooter. He won't let you down." His nostrils flared as he blew smoke from them. "I know you have a lot of questions to ask me, Mr. Rennert. Suppose, before you start, you tell me what you've learned. I know that you found this fellow Voice's skeleton among those museum specimens. That's about all."

"Really, that about sums up the situation." Rennert proceeded to recount his activities since young Crockett had stepped into his office that hot afternoon. He concluded with the identification of the skeleton as that of Professor Voice and the report of the ballistic expert that the bullet found in the skull was that of a 32 caliber revolver.

Roark listened intently.

"What became of Biggerstaff?" he asked.

"I brought him back in the plane with me," Rennert told him. "He's at the American Hospital now, getting an examination."

"What did you learn from him?"

"Not a great deal. He's still suffering from the effects of that blow on the head, and the doctor thought it best not to worry him with questions. He seems to be at a complete loss to account for the presence of the skeleton in that shipment. He says there are two other members of this excavating party. Dr. Fogarty, the head, and a young man named Weikel. Know them?"

"I've met them. Fogarty's a gruff, kind-hearted old fellow. Weikel I never got to know. He looks like an unpleasant sort of

chap. All of them were formerly at Southwestern University, I believe. Fogarty as a member of the faculty, Biggerstaff and Weikel
as students." He shook his head slowly. "It's a puzzler, all right. I
made a discreet inquiry at the Department of Archaeology. Didn't
tell them, of course, what was up. They said that the shipment was
in order when their inspector gave the permit. His name is Diego
Echave, by the way. All three skeletons came from under the
Pedregal, the lava flow behind the Faudree house. They weren't
greatly interested in the Teague expedition, since they have been
finding very few valuable things."

"That's strange. I understood from Biggerstaff that they had
been having a very profitable winter. But suppose we get on with
your story now. I'd like to hear about those letters. Any personal
information about Voice would be helpful too."

Roark stared in absorption at the thick-napped green rug.

"It was on the twenty-ninth day of April that Voice came to the
embassy," he said. "Soon after we opened, on Wednesday morning. The old man called me in and introduced us. He was anxious
to get rid of Voice, who'd come without an appointment and talked
his way in. I brought him in here and had him tell me about the
letters. I could see that he was really frightened. He had received
the second one that morning. The first one came two days before.
Both of them were mailed in San Angel. But I have them here, if
you'd like to see them."

Roark strode around the desk to a metal filing cabinet and
pulled open one of the drawers.

"About Voice," he said over his shoulder as he sorted out the
manila folders with nimble fingers. "He was a typical college professor who goes in for research. About forty-five or fifty. Unmar-
ried. Frail, stoop-shouldered and bleached-looking. Wore gold-
rimmed glasses which he kept taking off and polishing all the time.
Spoke with a precise voice that got rather shrill when he became
excited. He was excited that morning, both on account of the letters and the *tecolotes*, the owls. Said he hadn't had any sleep in
several nights."

Roark located the folder and took out two envelopes. "Here we are."

Rennert seemed on the point of asking a question but reconsidered and gave his attention to the envelopes.

They were of the ordinary sort, which can be bought for a few centavos in any stationery store in Mexico. On them were printed in precise letters the words "Prof. Garnett Voice," with an address.

Rennert took a single sheet of notepaper from the one whose cancellation showed the prior date. He noted as he did so that the flap had been torn open carelessly or hastily, leaving jagged edges. The paper was of the same quality as the envelope, and the printing was similar to that of the superscription. He read:

> My frend, I need 10 thoussand pesos. Get them
> in silver and have them reddy when I call for them.
> Keep this to yourself. If you don't . . .

The rest of the page was devoted to a gruesome account of the fate which would befall Voice. There were four drawings, painstakingly made.

In the lower right-hand corner was a splattered blood-red drop in place of a signature.

Roark had been following the course of Rennert's eyes. "Mercurochrome," he said. "I had it examined."

Rennert nodded and went on to the second letter.

> Bring the 10 thoussand pesos to the Pedregal tomorrow nite. There are 3 tal cacti in a direck line with the south window of your room. Each nite at midnight you will do this: Walk to the first cactus and wait 5 minutes. If you hear nothing go on to the second cactus and wait 5 minutes. If you hear nothing go to the third cactus and wait 5 minutes. Keep this up each nite at the same time. If you are alone I will call you and tell you to lay down the money. Don't tell anybody about this and don't fail to bring the money. If you don't—well, look here. . . .

There were more drawings, done with elaborate attention to detail. In each instance Voice was represented as a large figure, stark naked, with exaggerated buttocks, while his tormentor was a tiny thing with a body composed of straight lines and a spade-shaped head, whose thick lips were set in an evil snicker.

Rennert took the letters in turn, scrutinizing them carefully, particularly the drawings. At last he laid them on his lap and sat staring at them. There was a discernible tightening of the corners of his lips.

"Well," Roark asked, "what do you make of them?"

When Rennert didn't reply at once, he went on:

"I've never had any experience with this sort of thing, but I showed them to a member of the staff here who is something of an expert on handwriting. He pointed out that the misspellings were a little obvious. 'Frend,' 'thoussand,' 'tal,' and so forth. And 'nite,' but 'midnight.' He mentioned, too, the correct plural of 'cactus,' which few people use. His opinion was that an educated person wrote the letters."

"Yes," Rennert was abstracted. "It's always difficult for an educated person to know what words an uneducated one would misspell. There's another thing—that figure 7. Would a Mexican make a 7 like that?"

Roark leaned over and glanced at the sheet.

"Of course not," he said almost at once. "He'd put a horizontal bar through it. They always do that to distinguish a 7 from a 1." He straightened up and looked hard at Rennert's face. "You agree, then, that it must have been an educated person who wrote those letters? Probably an American?"

"Yes." Rennert's thoughts were elsewhere. "And one who prints deftly. Do you mind if I keep these for a time?"

"Of course not." Roark's face was very sober now, drawn into lines which made him look older. "At the time Voice showed me those letters I thought somebody was playing a joke on him. He was so frightened by the *tecolotes* that he was ready to jump at his own shadow. But since I heard that you had discovered his body, that he had been murdered, I've been doing some thinking."

He hesitated and kept his gaze fixed on the rug. "I'm not putting any stock in the melodramatic bandit idea. There aren't any of them in the Pedregal. But isn't it possible that there is an up-to-date band of extortionists operating here in Mexico City? The newspapers give so much space to the work of extortionists in the United States that it'd be surprising if someone didn't get the idea of imitating them." His eyes were keener now as they rose hopefully to Rennert's face.

"That's a theory which we'll have to consider," the latter said. "But go ahead and tell me what you did after Voice visited you."

"Well, looking back on it now, I can see that I didn't do much. I went out to San Angel with him and had a look around the Pedregal. Sure enough, there are three cacti in a line with his window, so whoever wrote the letters must have known the ground. I talked to the members of the Teague party and the Faudrees. None of them had anything helpful in the way of information. I don't think they took Voice and his fears very seriously."

"All of them knew about the letters, then?"

"Oh yes. I judged that Voice had appealed to everyone for help in watching the Pedregal for suspicious characters."

"Are you sure that John Biggerstaff knew about them?"

"Yes. I remember talking with him."

"What comment did he make?"

Roark thought for a moment. "He just laughed and said that he didn't think there was anything for Voice to worry about, that no bandit worthy of the name was going to waste time trying to get money out of a college professor when there were so many better prospects."

"Not a bad point. Did you learn anything about Voice's financial condition?"

"He told me at the beginning that he didn't have ten thousand pesos or he'd have taken it to the Pedregal and kept still. He was taking this year off from the university without pay, and his savings were just about used up."

There was a slight narrowing of Roark's eyes. "Biggerstaff didn't tell you about these letters?"

"No, but, as I said, I talked to him very little."

"But you'd have thought they would have come to his mind at once when he heard that Voice had been murdered, wouldn't you?"

"Yes."

There was a momentary silence.

"That ended your investigation at San Angel?" Rennert asked.

"Yes." Roark brought his attention back. "I stayed there that night with Voice, but nothing happened. Except," he said in an odd voice, "the *tecolotes*. There were a lot of them." He went on hurriedly, "No letter came the next morning, so I left. I told Voice to call me the next time one came. I talked to the police, but they knew of no one in the vicinity who might be writing the letters. They ridiculed the idea of kidnapers. I came on back to the embassy then. I called up the Faudree house several days later and asked for Voice. I wanted to be sure he was all right. But I was told that he had gone back to the United States."

This interested Rennert. "Was any explanation made of this sudden trip?"

"No." Roark glanced at his watch. "Do you want to go out to San Angel this afternoon?"

"Yes, if it's convenient."

"I'll call and find out." Roark swung a receiver from its cradle and spoke to the switchboard operator.

"If we start now we can look over the excavations before the rain starts," he said as he waited. "You know Mexico well enough to expect the daily showers in the summer, don't you?"

"Yes. I may forget anything else down here, but not my raincoat. It's in the hall."

Rennert had risen and strolled nearer the desk.

Facing the typewriter was a small picture frame of black leather on a base of milky-gray onyx. The photograph in it was, he felt sure, that of the girl whose face had looked out at him from Biggerstaff's billfold. She was younger here, undoubtedly, but at the same time less attractive. Her hair was close-cropped like a boy's; her eyes were darker and lusterless; her mouth hard and cynical. She wore what looked like an artist's smock. Photography alone couldn't account for the difference. . . .

"What are the names of the Faudree sisters and their niece?" he asked.

"Lucy and Monica are the sisters. Cornell's the niece. Lucy and Monica are of a certain age, as the French say."

"And Cornell?"

"Oh, in her early thirties, I think. Thanks." Roark replaced the receiver.

He was frowning slightly as he turned to Rennert. "Something's wrong with the Faudree phone. Line seems to be disconnected. I suppose we might as well go on out, though. I don't think Lucy ever leaves the house."

Rennert watched him fit a gray felt hat snugly onto his head. "I'm not taking you away from your duties, am I?"

"Lord no. I haven't any duties here as long as you require my services. To tell the truth, this assignment is more to my liking than most I draw. It's better than escorting some visiting politician and his wife about to tea parties."

"I hope you're not counting on too much in the way of excitement. I'll probably do nothing but ask questions."

A glint of shrewdness came into Roark's eyes. "I noticed your face while you were looking at those letters, Mr. Rennert. You saw something you weren't satisfied with."

Rennert stared past him into the sunlight. "I saw something I didn't like," he admitted.

"Nothing about them is exactly pleasant."

"Oh, it's not the wording or the melodramatic blood spot. It's the drawings, the sadism they show. Someone must have spent hours and hours on them, vicariously mutilating this professor."

A muscle twitched along Roark's smooth-shaven jaw. "Voice wasn't mutilated when you found him, was he?"

"We only saw the skeleton. It wouldn't show on that." Rennert paused and said slowly, "And the figures on those drawings remind me of something. I can't recall what. Somewhere I've seen similar ones. It bothers me."

Roark's hand tightened on the doorknob. "I know what they remind me of. Things I saw scratched on the walls of a cell in San Juan de Ulúa. Some poor devil 'd been imprisoned there, below sea level. He'd spent months making pictures of what he'd like to do to his jailers."

Rennert nodded. "We'll probably find that the person who drew these pictures is in a prison, though it's only a mental one."

6
SOUTH

A DOCTOR AT THE American Hospital who has grown old attending to the ills of his countrymen resident and transient in Mexico said to Rennert:

"Mr. Biggerstaff's condition is not serious, provided he allows himself time for recuperation. Ordinarily I should recommend that he stay here, but he is so insistent on returning to San Angel that I'm going to allow him to do so. An enforced stay would probably only make him restless. He has a strong constitution, and the injury to his head should leave no permanent effects. He seems to have a great deal of faith in you, Mr. Rennert. Will you undertake to look over the living conditions at the house where he is staying and urge someone there to see that he is subjected to no mental or physical strain for a week or so?"

Rennert hesitated. There was no telling what might develop in that house at San Angel. "Yes," he said finally.

"Very well then."

The doctor spoke into a telephone: "Send Mr. Biggerstaff in, please."

He turned back to Rennert. "I don't want to alarm Mr. Biggerstaff, but there are certain potentially dangerous possibilities in his case. The human brain is a delicate organ and a mysterious one. At an unexpected moment it may lose its balance wheel, so to speak. Do you know anything about the circumstances of his previous head injury?"

"No. I did notice the scar on his forehead."

"I asked him about that, but he said he had received it in a fall years ago and that it had never bothered him. We'll trust that such will be the case with this."

The door opened, and Biggerstaff came in, grip and hat in his left hand. His right was carried in a sling. The bandage which covered the right side of his head made his smile look strained. He was rather pale beneath his tan.

"Well, Mr. Rennert," he said eagerly, "have you convinced him that I was in my right mind on the trip down here? I've had the idea that someone's been watching me all the time I've been here to see if I didn't start gibbering."

"See here, young man," the doctor said severely, "I'm going to let you go under your promise to obey my instructions. No working for at least two weeks. Come back in three days and let me look you over. Don't stay up for more than an hour longer today. Take two of those sedative tablets I gave you and go to bed. You'll sleep till morning. Is that clear?"

"Yes sir, I'll take care of myself." Biggerstaff looked at Rennert. "Ready to go, Mr. Rennert?"

"And remember," the doctor said finally, "that I'm empowering Mr. Rennert to send you back here if you get obstreperous."

"Yes sir."

As they walked toward the waiting embassy car Biggerstaff said, "So you're still having to look after me, Mr. Rennert. I sure appreciate it, but you don't need to worry about me. I'll be all right now."

"Remember . . ." Rennert said significantly.

"Yes, I will. But none of you realize how hard the old Biggerstaff head is." An expression of surprise crossed his face. "Oh, hello, Mr. Roark! Glad to see you again."

He shook hands cordially with the attaché and at his direction gave the grip to the serious-faced Mexican chauffeur to place on the front seat. Roark moved over in the rear to let them in, told the driver their destination and sank back on the cushions as they started.

"Some difference between my departure from San Angel and my return," Biggerstaff laughed. "I went away in a truck, sitting on a packing case, and I come back—between the State and the Treasury departments of the United States."

He was patently self-conscious. His big fingers kept turning his hat about on his lap as his black eyes went from one of their faces to the other. Roark, smoking and staring almost moodily out into the sunlight, did not seem disposed to put him at his ease. His attitude almost gave the effect of hostility.

Rennert told himself that he was being imaginative. Biggerstaff's hips were wide, considering his slender body, so that the three of them were wedged rather tightly in the back seat.

The atmosphere was uncomfortably warm and dense, charged with electrical portent of the storm clouds which were advancing from all sides upon the valley, trailing their dark curtains of rain. Rennert's clothing was moist with perspiration, and the raincoat which he had folded over his knee stuck irritatingly to his fingers.

Biggerstaff shifted his position, as if trying to give the others more room.

"Mr. Rennert," he said hesitantly, "I don't suppose I ought to ask any questions, but I would like to know whether you've found out anything—about Professor Voice."

"I haven't any objection to telling you, Biggerstaff. The principal thing I've learned is about those extortion letters that he received."

"Oh, those!" Biggerstaff started to laugh but checked himself. The thick black brows which gave his eyes such a deep-set effect drew together in a frown. "Do you think they were real?" There was a note of incredulity in his voice.

"It looks as if they were, doesn't it? I judge that you didn't think so."

"Why no, I didn't take them seriously at all. I remember when Mr. Roark came out to investigate them." He stared fixedly at the upholstery of the front seat as if something were troubling him.

"Who did you think was writing them?"

Biggerstaff's fingers tugged at the hatbrim. "I thought somebody was playing a joke on Mr. Voice. You did too, didn't you?" he asked defensively of Roark.

The latter nodded, and a slight smile broke the tension of his face.

"A hell of detective I was," he said shortly.

"Did Voice have many acquaintances?" Rennert asked.

"No, hardly any."

"Then it must not have been difficult for you to pick out the joker."

Biggerstaff swallowed, the prominent Adam's apple which met his collar making the action more noticeable. "I thought I did know."

Rennert's silence was a question.

"But if the person who wrote them really did have anything to do with Voice's death," Biggerstaff hurried on, "then I was wrong. I'm sure I was wrong," he said almost fiercely, as if to drive conviction home to himself.

They turned off Artes into the broad avenue of the Insurgents, which shoots southward to San Angel.

"Listen, Mr. Rennert!" Biggerstaff turned to him and made a motion with his hand as if to catch his sleeve. "I want to help you all I can. But I'd rather not tell you who I thought it was. It was nothing but a suspicion, you see. But if you decide that those letters did have some connection with this other— I'll tell you. Is that all right?"'

"We'll let it go at that, Biggerstaff."

"Thanks." The young man stared for a moment at the rococo villas and green lawns which Hank this street. The grass and the bougainvillaea climbing over blue and ocher and salmon-pink plaster walls looked unreal in the glassy air.

"I suppose you'll talk to everybody out at the Faudrees'?" he asked.

Rennert smiled. "I should prefer, of course, that they talked to me."

"Yes, surely. But what I was thinking was—" Biggerstaff hesitated and went on in some confusion—"that maybe I'd better tell you something about them. The Faudrees, I mean. So as to sort of prepare you."

"I'll be glad to hear anything you want to tell me."

Biggerstaff passed his hand across his forehead as if it pained him.

"They're awfully nice people, once you get to know them. A very famous family. There are these sisters, Lucy and Monica, and their

niece Cornell. Cornell's mother and father were killed in an accident when she was very young, and she made her home with her
grandfather. Since his death she has continued to live with her
aunts. Tindall Faudree, the founder of the family in Mexico, was a
cavalry leader in the Civil War."

He talked on, with a didacticism which gave way to his enthu-
siasm, about Colonel Faudree's participation in the war and in the
events which followed, when he and men like him turned their eyes
southward to drown the bitterness of defeat in mad and grandiose
plans for new commonwealths. When Kirby-Smith held the border and Maximilian's empire flickered out in a rain of blood.
Biggerstaff was well grounded in history, Rennert realized at once,
and had caught the romantic spirit of the time. . . .

It wasn't until they were passing through the streets of Mixcoac
that he fell silent.

The driver had moderated his speed, and Rennert could see the
tops of eucalyptus, ash and laurel trees above the glass walls of
the Botanical Gardens. From a slope there, he remembered, one
could gaze without obstacle at Popocatepetl and his White Lady,
at Mount Ajusco and the orchards of San Angel. That is, if one's
business in Mexico weren't to hunt down a murderer. . . .

"You have to understand that background," Biggerstaff said
judicially, "to understand Lucy and Monica. Especially Lucy. She's
terribly proud and lives in the past. The other families who came
down here from the South have given up their isolation and inter-
married with Mexicans or other Americans. But not Lucy! 'Unconquered' is the motto on the Faudree coat of arms." He smiled. "She's
still waving the rebel flag."

The smile lingered, and his voice took on a gentler note.
"Cornell, now, is different. She says that she's not going to be bound
by a lot of musty traditions. She's sensible. She's independent.
She's enterprising. She's—"

He broke off and asked, "Do you know about the Mexican cus-
tom of willing the rooms in a house to different children?"

Rennert nodded. "I know how it complicates the buying or the
leasing of a house."

"Well, that's what Mr. Faudree, the father of Lucy and Monica, did. He wanted to make sure the house would stay in the family. He left the downstairs to Lucy and divided the upstairs between Monica and Cornell. He treated Cornell as one of his own daughters, you see. Each has full title to her part. And the house can't be sold without the consent of all three. Well, when Dr. Fogarty and Weikel and I came down last October we got permission to excavate on the grounds at the rear. The house being so handy and so large, we asked if we couldn't rent rooms there. Lucy and Monica wouldn't have dreamed of letting us, I know, but Cornell said we could have the three rooms which belonged to her. She fixed up the attic into an apartment for herself. It's a good arrangement, although Lucy—" his mouth twisted into a wry smile—"doesn't approve of us archaeologists. Or of Cornell's bringing us into the house. All modern scientists, to her mind, are a Godless crew."

He stopped abruptly and said into space, "I wonder what's wrong with their phone? I called from the hospital but couldn't get any answer."

They were whirled through the shaded plaza of San Angel, and turned to the south between walls of black volcanic stone almost hidden by bougainvillaea. Iron gates gave kaleidoscopic glimpses of painted doorways and flowers in a tropical profusion of color. They passed the crumbling towers of the Carmelite church.

Had he been transported there blindfolded, Rennert thought, he would have known that he was in San Angel. The smell of the place would have told him. For, more pervasive now through the cloying aroma of the flowers, his nostrils recognized the dank odor of decay. It is no gardener's skill which fills San Angel with flowers. Here, perhaps longer than in any other spot on the continent, man has lived and died and with his disintegration given additional fertility to the dark soil. The cycle goes on, and each year the flowers of San Angel take on brighter hues, fill the air with heavier perfume. . . .

Biggerstaff sat forward, his free hand grasping the rear of the front seat, and gazed ahead. His eyes sparkled with excitement, and Rennert could hear his breathing quicken.

They left the paved street and turned onto a narrow, rutted

causeway which paralleled a shallow stream of running water. The thick grass almost concealed the ancient flat stones with which the path was flagged.

Suddenly Biggerstaff gestured ahead and to the left.

"There's the Pedregal," he announced.

Through a breach in a wall Rennert had a glimpse of it: a stormy sea whose black viscous waves had been halted suddenly by petrifaction. Sunlight bathed it near at hand, lending a certain wild beauty to the dead surface torn by chasms and queer whirlpools where the impotent fury of the cataclysm had vented itself. Its confines were lost in the mists which were gathering about Mount Ajusco, fourteen miles away.

Biggerstaff's young homely face wore a rapt expression, and his voice had a possessive quality, as if he were displaying some domain of his own to these visitors.

"There's the volcano, extinct now, of course. It erupted over two thousand years ago. And there's the lava, just as it cooled. Grand, isn't it! Somebody has said it's like seeing the surface of the moon through a telescope. And sealed down underneath are the bones of the people who lived here then, their pottery and weapons, their pyramids and cemeteries—"

He hit the driver's shoulder.

"Stop, will you? Stop!" It was almost a shout.

Ahead of them a girl, going in the same direction as they, had turned aside at the sound of the car. She was a slender girl in a blue knitted skirt and suede jacket. Her head was bare, and the sunlight brought out the golden tints in her loose chestnut hair. She was carrying a number of packages.

Biggerstaff had clambered over Roark's feet and opened the door almost before the driver brought the car to a standstill.

"Cornell!"

The girl whirled about, her lips parted by surprise, and when she saw who it was gave a little cry:

"John!"

Her face went pale as her eyes rested on the bandage about his head. "John, what's happened?"

Biggerstaff sprang to the ground and went to her. He held his left hand raised, awkwardly, as if he didn't know what to do with it.

"Turbans are in style up in Texas, so I thought I'd get me one." He laughed and poked the white cloth with a finger. "How do you like it?"

"But, John, be serious—tell me what's happened to you."

"A little train wreck, that's all. I tried to ram my head through a wall but couldn't quite make it. Nothing to be worried about."

Her eyes stayed on his face for a moment, searchingly, as if she wished to assure herself that each feature was as before. The color began to come back into her cheeks, and she turned to the car.

She looked straight at Roark, and Rennert had the fleeting impression that she steeled herself.

"Hello, Delaney. It's good to see you again." Despite the casual friendliness of her manner there was some undercurrent of emotion there which she could not entirely repress.

"Hello, Cornell." Roark's voice was perfectly steady, his eyes meeting hers without a flicker to disturb their cool, tired gaze. But on the side of his mouth turned to Rennert a muscle twitched before his lips took on a hard, almost cynical set.

The whole incident was as intangible as the faint humming of a tautened wire. It was probably as unimportant. Rennert wasn't sure that he understood it.

Biggerstaff didn't seem to notice it. He was like nothing so much as a healthy, happy puppy, full of meat and irrepressible spirits. His face was beaming as he caught Cornell's arm and drew her up to the side of the car.

"Miss Faudree, I want to present Mr. Rennert. He's of the United States Customs Service. He's been—well, a kind of nursemaid to me. Brought me down in the plane with him. I know you'll like him."

The girl's eyes rested on Rennert's face for the first time. They were of deep hazel, their gaze clear and penetrating. The high bridge of her nose, and her eyebrows, a shade darker than her hair, gave them a certain boldness.

She extended a hand, and her clasp was as forthright as a man's. "I'm sure I shall. Tell me about John, won't you, Mr. Rennert? Is he really all right?"

"As he says, there's nothing to worry about. He is going to have to take a rest, that's all."

"A rest?" She turned. "Oh then, John, you were really hurt. You oughtn't to joke about it. You might have been killed."

Biggerstaff laughed carelessly. "Forget it. Let me have those bundles, then get in the car. We'll drive home in state. It's not every day you get to ride in a car from the United States Embassy."

He helped her into the seat between Roark and Rennert, then wormed himself into the front, the grip between his knees.

There was a moment of silence as they started on. Rennert could see a slightly puzzled expression come over the girl's face as she stole a glance at first one and then the other of the men beside her.

He said, "We are on our way to call at your house, Miss Faudree. I'm glad that Mr. Biggerstaff has seen fit to vouch for me, although he has exaggerated my services. I wonder if you have time to talk to Mr. Roark and myself this afternoon?"

"Why, of course. I haven't thanked you yet for helping John, but I was going to. You must come up to my apartment."

Biggerstaff had turned about. "Mr. Rennert has some news that's going to surprise you, Cornell. You remember Professor Voice?"

"Yes."

"Well, it's about him." He looked at Rennert. "Shall I tell her, Mr. Rennert?"

"Since you have her curiosity aroused, yes."

"Well," Biggerstaff said excitedly, "Voice was murdered. Somebody shot him and put his body in place of one of those skeletons that I was taking to the border."

"Murdered?" She stared at him, then turned to Rennert. "Is he joking, Mr. Rennert?"

"No, Miss Faudree. It's the truth."

"But when—when did this happen?"

"About the first of May, I think."

Her eyes still held his, but a cloudiness came into them. "Then Mr. Voice didn't go away?"

"No, he didn't go away."

"But his note!" she exclaimed suddenly. "I wonder why he sent that?"

"You received a note from him?"

"Yes. Lucy, my aunt, did, rather. I didn't see it. But I understood that he said he was called away unexpectedly to the United States."

"It came through the mail?"

"Yes."

"When was this?"

"Over a month ago. It must have been about the first of May. Aunt Lucy will remember."

Rennert had the feeling that some belated consideration was forcing itself into her thoughts, cooling the natural spontaneity of her manner.

His next question was forestalled by Biggerstaff, who had turned his head and spoken to the driver. The latter brought the car to an abrupt stop beside a gnarled eucalyptus tree which blocked further progress in this direction.

Cornell's laugh was nervous. "But come in. As we say in Mexico, here you have your house."

7
GUN

THE HOUSE STOOD against a background starkly Mexican: cold volcanoes and black lava and pine-covered mountains shrouded in rain. Low stone walls, their crumblings masked by bougain-villaea, marked the confines of its extensive grounds. Its materials were dark stones whose only names are Aztec: *tepetate* and the igneous *tezontle*. They gave an incongruous effect to the effort at Georgian architecture—the two long stories with a roof set with dormer windows sloping back to the height of another, the faded green shutters, the white-painted wooden pillars which supported the roof of a small porch.

As Rennert walked toward it up a gravel path bordered by sea shells, he was impressed by the sense of isolation which came over him. Not a quarter of a mile away were the villas and streets of San Angel. But no sound of their activity came to this place. It was as if the house partook of some of the qualities of the dead acres of stone behind it.

Biggerstaff was whistling a low, rollicking tune as he sprang up the steps. He dropped the grip, took a key from his pocket and unlocked the front door.

They entered a hall in whose spaces a few articles of furniture—a low love seat cushioned in satin, a few high-backed Spanish chairs, a tall pendulum clock, a hat-rack—seemed lost.

Opposite the door rose a wide staircase.

"You can leave your hats and coats here," Biggerstaff told them, nodding toward the rack.

As they made their way up the heavily carpeted treads Rennert's eyes took in something of the arrangement of the house. A narrow ill-lit transverse hall met the larger one at right angles to the stairway. Halfway up was a landing, from which another flight descended to what was evidently a rear door.

He heard Cornell say to Biggerstaff, "John, there's a letter for you. It's in your room."

"From the museum?"

"Yes."

As they emerged into a wide corridor, laid with coco matting, Biggerstaff turned to Rennert and Roark. His voice trembled a bit. "Excuse me, will you? Cornell will take you upstairs."

He walked with quick steps toward a room directly across the hall.

Cornell led the way to the right, opened one of two doors at the end of the hall and preceded them up a steep flight of uncarpeted stairs.

They found themselves in a long room, with walls and ceiling of buff beaverboard. There were many windows, enlivened by gay chintz curtains. The furnishings were old and ill-assorted, but a certain color scheme had been worked out by means of slip covers and cushions. There were flowers.

She relieved them of the packages. "Sit down, won't you?"

Roark had brought out a package of cigarettes. He started to take one, then looked at her and said: "I suppose you still refuse?"

"Yes," she said evenly, "I still refuse." She turned to Rennert. "Tell me the truth, Mr. Rennert, about John. What did the doctor really say?"

Rennert started to tell her.

Before he had gone beyond a few words the door at the foot of the stairs slammed, and Biggerstaff came bounding up. A smile broadened his lips, and his eyes were bright with excitement. He was waving a letter in his left hand.

"I got it, dear! I got it!"

"Oh, John!" Cornell went to meet him. "Let me see!"

Her hand trembled as she ran her eyes over the sheet of paper. She folded it, and their eyes met.

"I've been waiting for you to come back and open it," she said unsteadily. "I was sure what it'd be but I was afraid. I've looked at that envelope, felt it—tried to make it tell me what was in it. I knew it couldn't be anything but good news. Now . . ." She stopped, color mounting to her cheeks.

"Now . . ." he repeated.

She raised a hand to brush back her hair, laughed self-consciously and turned to Rennert and Roark. "Oh, please pardon us! We—we don't often act this way. But John's just got some good news. Tell them, John."

Biggerstaff took a deep breath and rested his weight first on one foot and then on the other. He made an effort to speak calmly.

"It's a letter from the Teague Museum in Sari Antonio. I put in an application for a job on their permanent staff this spring. And—well, I got it."

As the two men murmured polite congratulations, he went on:

"You probably don't realize how much this means to me. It's something I've been working for so long. I've got a chance now to do some real work in archaeology, something more than just wielding a pick."

There was a pause, and for the first time constraint crept into the atmosphere of the room. There was, Rennert knew, nothing more he and Roark could say with regard to the young man's good fortune. They could only sit there, reminders of another matter which waited to be discussed.

Cornell must have realized this, for she caught Biggerstaff's arm and drew him from the center of the room. "Sit down, John. Mr. Rennert and Mr. Roark haven't come here to hear us talk about ourselves."

She sank into a wicker basket chair, while Biggerstaff dropped onto a low hassock close by.

"Now, Mr. Rennert," she said, "tell us about Mr. Voice. I haven't given him a thought in over a month. Suddenly to hear that—he's dead, in this way—well, it's hard to grasp. Tell me about him, please."

She sat listening with a slowly deepening frown as he told of the discovery of the skeleton at the border and of its identification as that of the university professor.

Biggerstaff, on the other hand, did not appear to be listening. His legs were spread wide apart, and he was leaning back, staring out the window.

When Rennert had concluded, the girl's face relaxed somewhat and she sank back in the chair. "It's fantastic. Mr. Voice was such a harmless soul, all wrapped up in his work. He couldn't have had an enemy anywhere, I'd have thought."

Her gaze had been wandering from place to place about the room. Suddenly it stopped, on a blue-and-white Talavera vase which held a mass of pink carnations.

"John!" She turned swiftly. "Those letters!"

An expression of pain or of displeasure passed over Biggerstaff's face. He did not look at her but squirmed slightly on the leather cushion.

"Mr. Rennert asked me about them. I told him that I'd never taken them seriously. I don't know what to think now."

The flush had entirely left Cornell's cheeks.

"Oh, this is terrible!" She glanced at Roark. "What do you think, Mr. Roark? You saw them."

(Rennert noted that only in her first greeting had she addressed him as Delaney.)

Roark did not answer for a moment. He seemed disconcerted by the question.

"At the time," he said a bit stiffly, "I thought as Biggerstaff—that someone was playing a joke on Voice. It seems that I was mistaken."

"You think that someone *did* kill him because he didn't pay the money?"

Roark only shrugged.

Rennert said, "You think, then, Miss Faudree, that Mr. Voice wasn't going to pay?"

"No. He didn't have that much money." Her eyes were troubled as they tried to attract those of Biggerstaff.

The latter was staring at the floor and refused to look up. There was an obstinate set to his jaw and compressed lips which made him look older, not at all like the ebullient boy who had come dashing up the stairs a few minutes before.

"There's another question which I must ask, Miss Faudree," Rennert said. "Did Professor Voice have a gun?"

"No, I don't think so." She glanced for confirmation at first Biggerstaff, then Roark.

The former shook his head.

"He told me that he didn't," Roark said. "I offered to loan him mine, but he refused. Said that he'd never handled a gun in his life."

Rennert turned to the girl again. "What other guns are there in the house, Miss Faudree?"

She thought for a moment. "I don't think there are any. Except an old one I have."

"Might I see it?"

"Why certainly." She seemed surprised. "It's one that belonged to my father."

She got up and went to a carved chest in the corner. It was several minutes before she came back with a revolver held on the palm of her hand.

Rennert took it and examined it perfunctorily. It was a 32 caliber revolver of an obsolete make. There were two shells in its chambers.

"You keep it loaded," he commented.

"Oh, I'm responsible for that," Biggerstaff interposed. "I've borrowed it once or twice to practice on targets out in the Pedregal. I left those shells in it because—well, because I thought Cornell ought to have some protection out here. Our party will be going back to the United States before long. And this house is so isolated."

"May I borrow this, Miss Faudree?" Rennert asked.

"Why of course," she said readily. "There's no need for me to keep it at all. I've told John that I'd be perfectly safe."

"You've never been bothered by thieves or vagrants?"

"Never. San Angel's a peaceable place."

As Rennert slipped the revolver into a hip pocket he saw Biggerstaff's eyes follow the movement. Perhaps it was the light glinting on their pupils which gave them their took of sharpness.

Rennert glanced at his watch and rose.

"Well, Biggerstaff, we're forgetting the doctor's orders. They apply to a member of the Teague Museum staff as well as to a simple wielder of a pick."

The young man flung back his head. "Oh, Mr. Rennert, I don't feel like going to bed yet." He forced a grin. "I've just got here—and Cornell and I've got some things we want to say to each other. The doctor's hour isn't up yet."

"You have about twenty minutes," Rennert admitted. "I want to look around a bit. When I get through I'll come back to see that you're tucked in and have taken that sedative. You'll make him behave in the meantime, Miss Faudree?"

"I certainly will, Mr. Rennert." The girl got to her feet and said hesitantly, "You'll want to see my aunts, I suppose?"

"If it's convenient."

"Aunt Lucy will be downstairs. I can take you down and introduce you."

Rennert remembered Biggerstaff's words about the strained relationship between Cornell and her relatives. "That's not necessary, Miss Faudree. Mr. Roark can introduce me."

She didn't succeed in hiding her relief. "If you will, Mr. Roark. Just go into the living room—the parlor, we call it—and ring for Marta, the maid. She'll call Aunt Lucy."

"Thank you. We'll turn the patient over to you now."

As they went down the stairs Rennert glanced at Roark's face.

"Love," he said, "must have its way, even with a doctor's orders."

The cynicism was on Roark's lips again. "My God, Rennert, are you going to get lyrical about it? I suppose you left them there so they could bill and coo without being inhibited by our presence?"

Rennert smiled. "To tell the truth, I left them there so they could make up their minds whether or not to tell me about those letters."

"You think they know who wrote them?"

"I think they do."

8
GOLD

FROM THE HALL they entered a huge high-ceilinged room already dim with twilight. Heavy dark draperies masked windows which, judging by the faintly musty odor, were seldom opened to sunlight.

As Roark stopped by the door to pull a red velvet bell-cord, Rennert's eyes wandered over the polished formal furniture, the harpsichord of satinwood and French walnut, the chandelier with cut-crystal drops, the large fireplace, the gilt-framed portrait above it.

Roark's voice sounded hushed: "Tindall Faudree, the grandfather."

He turned his head. "Oh hello, Marta. Is Miss Lucy in?"

The woman on the threshold had appeared so silently that only a rustle of skirts had betrayed her presence.

Her features seemed finer than those of most mulattoes, the lips not conspicuously thick. Her black hair, drawn tightly back to the nape of her neck, was made attractive rather than otherwise by its slight kinkiness. A gold bracelet dangling heavily on her right wrist was a bright, barbaric note in the gloom.

Her "Yes" was low, with a toneless quality, as if she were speaking an unaccustomed language.

"I wonder if we might see her?" Roark drew a card from his billfold.

She took it, then the one which Rennert produced. "In a moment," she said, and was gone.

The two men waited in silence, as if a reverent constraint were implicit in the atmosphere of the room.

Rennert compared this with the gay, many-windowed apartment upstairs.

He followed Roark's example and tried one of the chairs which stood in stiff alignment before the fireplace. It creaked slightly under his not inconsiderable weight. He began to inspect it unobtrusively, wondering if it were, as it seemed, a genuine Chippendale. It was a habit which his profession had ingrained in him—to test and evaluate every object with which he came in contact. If people, he had often thought, were only as easily understood as things!

It was a habit which often proved embarrassing, he told himself as he straightened up at the opening of the door.

A small woman in black satin entered. She paused for a second, then came toward them, a black ebony cane padding softly on the rug.

"Mr. Roark, this is a pleasure." She smiled as she extended a hand.

"The pleasure is certainly mine, Miss Faudree. May I present Mr. Rennert?"

"Mr. Rennert." He felt cool slender fingers touch his for an instant as keen black eyes scrutinized his face. He hoped that his bow approached the ease and urbanity of the young diplomat's.

"Welcome to our home," she said. "Won't you gentlemen be seated?"

As she went toward a brocaded armchair a little distance away, Marta came quietly into the room and began lighting the tall wax candles on the mantel.

As their soft light flowed out Rennert said:

"I have been admiring your fireplace, Miss Faudree. One seldom sees nowadays such a happy combination of utility and beauty."

"Yes. It is a replica of the fireplace in the old Faudree plantation. My grandfather brought the mantelpiece with him to Mexico. The marble was carved in France."

It occupied the angle between the two doors. On either side of the yawning cavern of blackened bricks were huge andirons in the

shape of mythological monsters. Set into the front of the elabo-
rately carved mantel was a shield bearing heraldic figures. An arm
brandishing a sword and a single word: Invicti.

But she wasn't looking at the mantel.

Above the Bohemian glass wine bottles, alabaster statuettes and
framed daguerreotypes which shared its top with the mahogany
candlesticks was an oil portrait of a white-haired, white-mustached
man in a gray uniform. His bold, arrogant features were dominated
by piercing black eyes set far apart on either side of the bridge of a
Roman nose.

Two generations hadn't broken the mold, Rennert thought as
he looked at the woman who sat forward in her chair, a black cashmere shawl about her thin, erect shoulders, regarding the portrait
with proud eyes. Lucy's face was pale, so pale that it resembled
the dead-white fragility of a cameo. The candlelight made her thin,
impeccably arranged hair a cap of silver. The hair and the shut-in
pallor made it difficult to estimate her age. Probably not more than
sixty. Perhaps much less.

"A remarkable man," Rennert said. "Tindall Faudree's career
always interested me."

"He was a remarkable man," she said with a simple note of
pride. "His life was a combination of the two qualities you mentioned about the fireplace: utility and beauty." Her voice was soft,
somewhat like that of the maid who had slipped out soundlessly.
But it was the softness of Mexico, not that of the South above the
Rio Grande.

"I understand that Professor Garnett Voice was doing some
research on Colonel Faudree's life," Rennert said quietly.

"Yes." Her eyes sought his face, and there was a faint flicker of
curiosity in them. "He was copying some family letters, particularly those which dealt with his activities in the war and his migra-
tion to Mexico." She paused. "Do you know Professor Voice?"

"No, I don't."

"I thought perhaps you brought some message from him. It's
strange that he hasn't written or sent back for his papers since he
went to the United States. He seemed so interested in his work."

Rennert gauged the strength inherent in her face.

"You never considered the possibility that Mr. Voice might be unable to write"

"Unable to write? I don't understand, Mr. Rennert. You mean on account of illness?"

"More than illness, Miss Faudree. I mean death."

She did not move, but a shadow seemed to pass over her face, as if a hand had tilted the candles.

"I'm sorry," Rennert said, "that I must be the one to break the news. I understand that Professor Voice was related to you. You have my full sympathy."

Her fingers tightened their grip on the gold head of the cane.

"Please, Mr. Rennert—" her voice was perfectly steady—"do not think it necessary to temper the truth with consideration for me. Mr. Voice was a relative, as you say, but a distant one. He did not share the Faudree tradition as my sister and I know it. I see no need to pretend any great grief at his passing. But even if this were a shock to me, my words to you would be the same. A woman who has lived all her life in Mexico, as I have done, learns to face realities. You may speak to me as the head of the Faudree family, exactly as if I were a man."

When he had finished she leaned forward out of the shadows, so that every detail of her face was limned by the candlelight.

"Tell me how you know this."

He told her how identification had been made certain.

She sat motionless, her eyes fixed on his face. "You say he was murdered. It couldn't have been suicide, or accident, could it—with the lime?"

"Not very well, Miss Faudree."

"And it must have been done here, in San Angel, by the Pedregal?"

"All indications point to that."

There was a pause. Rennert wanted to go slowly here, letting her thoughts follow whatever line of speculation they were engaged upon.

But there was an interruption. Shoes squeaked faintly down the side hall and stopped outside the door. Lucy turned her head sharply to listen.

Just as the silence began to be prolonged unduly the door opened, and another woman came in. She stopped on the threshold, as Lucy had done, and coughed discreetly. Her long fingers played nervously over the ribbons and ruffles and bows of a black-and-white flowered chiffon dress.

In a flurried tone she said, "I wonder if I'm intruding."

There was an edge to Lucy's voice: "Come in, Monica. I should like to present Mr. Roark—and Mr. Rennert. This is my sister Monica, gentlemen."

"Oh, I know Mr. Roark. Of course I do. How are you, Mr. Roark?" She came into the room, raised her right hand uncertainly, checked it, then extended it.

"And Mr. Rennert. I am delighted, Mr. Rennert." He felt the fluttering tips of her fingers. She was no taller than he, but he felt a bit overwhelmed by so many yards of rippling goods, by so much towering hair. This was dark brown, almost black, and fluffy, as if it had been recently washed.

She was a woman several years younger than Lucy, and it had doubtless always been her fate to be considered plain, if not homely. Yet Rennert wondered if she hadn't missed a stately full-blown handsomeness by a rather narrow margin. Her brown eyes were large and luminous, despite the handicap of gold-rimmed glasses. The brows turned up slightly at the outer corners. Her mouth was wide and full but could never, he knew, soften to tenderness.

She was saying with increased exuberance:

"I know that I'm intruding. But I was up in Cornell's room and saw John—John Biggerstaff, that is. Lucy, did you know that he was back and that he'd been injured in a wreck?"

Lucy said with total lack of interest, "No." Monica turned her attention to Roark again. "I heard about the terrible discovery you men have made, so I had to come down and see you. And here is Mr. Roark, looking so severe, as if he had all sorts of state secrets on his mind. I know it must be a serious matter. But you can't deceive me, Mr. Roark. I know you have your lighter, more frivolous moments, just like everyone else. Now don't you?"

The young man contrived to keep his smile, but the corners of his mouth were tight.

"Of course," he said dryly.

"But it's all harmless, just relaxation from your duties, isn't it? That's what I told a friend of mine who was talking about the fast set that goes to the Foreign Club and other places to drink and gamble. She mentioned your name, but I told her—"

Lucy's voice cut in sharply: "If you want to sit down, Monica, please do so. Mr. Roark and Mr. Rennert aren't here to gossip."

"Oh yes, of course." She smoothed ineffectually at bunchy sleeves which did not come far enough down on her wrists. "If you really don't mind, I *will* sit down for a while. This news has been such a shock to me."

"You certainly don't act as if it had been a shock."

"Oh, but that's just a—well, a defense mechanism with me. To keep from thinking about it."

Rennert said, "We should be very glad to have you join our discussion, Miss Faudree. You may be of some assistance to us."

"I may? Then I shall stay, by all means."

While she was choosing a chair, Lucy addressed Rennert: "But do you know that Mr. Voice wrote me that he was going back to the United States?"

"When did you receive that letter?" he asked.

"Let's see. It was one of the first days in May."

"Did you notice where it was mailed?"

"In Mexico City, I believe."

"Oh!" The exclamation from Monica made them turn their heads. She was leaning forward, her face agitated, and pulling at the corners of a handkerchief.

"I know," she said. "It was written on May Day. It came on the second."

"How can you be so sure, Monica?" Lucy demanded.

"I—well, I just happen to remember."

"What were its contents, Miss Faudree?" Rennert had intended the question for Monica, but it was Lucy who answered.

"He said that he had been called away suddenly. He asked me to store his things for him, as he didn't know when he would return."

"The signature, I judge, appeared to be that of Professor Voice?"

Her gaze fell to the gigantic lotus flower which splashed the dark-green surface of the rug.

"The signature was typed," she said.

"The entire letter as well?"

"Yes."

"Did Voice own a typewriter?"

"Yes."

Rennert tried to repress the unwarranted excitement which was ready to quicken his voice. "Did you by any chance keep that letter, Miss Faudree?"

"No, I didn't."

Of course, after all these weeks it was too much to expect. Nevertheless he was disappointed.

He tried, unsuccessfully, to include both sisters in a question. "Did you know about the threatening letters which were sent to Professor Voice last April?"

"Why yes," Lucy said in evident surprise.

"Did you believe that they were written in all seriousness by an extortionist?"

"No." She considered for several seconds, then moved her head slowly back and forth. "Mr. Rennert, I know San Angel very well after a lifetime spent here. I know the people who live about the Pedregal. There have been times, during the Revolution, when such things might have happened. But now—I can't believe that there are any such criminals in the neighborhood."

"As far as I have ascertained, Mr. Voice received only two of these letters. Do you know if a third came just before his disappearance?"

"If so he said nothing about it."

"To your knowledge did he have any enemies here or elsewhere in Mexico?"

Her negative was more decisive. "No, none at all, I'm sure. He had very few acquaintances even, as far as I know. He was a simple, inoffensive man. I can conceive of no one wishing him harm."

"And you, Miss Faudree?" Rennert addressed Monica directly.

It seemed to take her a moment or two to comprehend the import of his words. She shook her head. "No, I don't think he had any enemies. But I had a premonition that something like this was going to happen."

"A premonition?" Rennert prompted.

"Yes. It was the *tecolotes*—the owls—out in the Pedregal. They made the most terrible noise with their hooting. Do you know what they say about the *tecolote* here in Mexico, Mr. Rennert?"

"Yes. The Indians consider it a harbinger of death. When was it you heard these *tecolotes*, Miss Faudree?" He glanced at Roark as he spoke. The latter was staring fixedly at Monica.

"Just before Mr. Voice went away," she said. "That is, before we thought he went away."

"While he was receiving those letters, then?"

"Yes."

Very low, although distinct, was the tapping of Lucy's cane. Her laughter rang across the room. "Mr. Rennert, you mustn't listen to Monica too credulously. Both she and Marta are overfond of their omens and apparitions and buried treasures. There are always *tecolotes* out in the Pedregal."

The handkerchief fluttered from Monica's fingers. Mechanically Roark rose and stooped to retrieve it. She took it from him absently.

"Maybe that's it!" Her voice was measured. "Maybe Mr. Voice found that treasure. Maybe somebody killed him to get it."

Lucy laughed derisively. "What utter nonsense, Monica! Mr. Rennert will take you for a simpleton."

Monica's jaw was set obstinately.

Her voice was low and evidently intended to be portentous. "What if I were to tell you that I've seen proof that there's a treasure buried between this house and the Pedregal?"

"Proof? You can't have seen any proof."

Monica dropped the handkerchief again.

"I have," she said. "One of the gold coins."

9
DUSK

LONG AFTER, Rennert's memory retained that picture: the meager yellow glow of the candles spreading fanlike into the darkening room, glittering back from Lucy's black eyes and seaming the handsome virile face which Roark kept upturned as he groped for the fallen handkerchief. In the utter silence which followed Monica's pronouncement leather creaked faintly upon the young man's person, his belt or one of his polished black shoes.

Incredulity, Rennert knew, was topmost in the minds of all three of them. If someone had laughed, smiled even, the spell would have been broken. But no one did. There had been something about the manner in which the words were spoken that carried too much conviction for that, but not enough for instant acceptance. Recollection of the momentary tableau was always to bring a wry smile to Rennert's lips. Not a glimmer of the simple, ironic truth came to the minds of any of that group as Monica went on speaking.

She was obviously enjoying the sensation which she had caused. She flashed Roark a gracious smile as he handed her the handkerchief.

"Yes." She seemed in no haste to proceed. "I saw one of the coins. Señor Echave, the Mexican who comes here to inspect the finds that these archaeologists make, was showing it to Marta the other day when I happened up. He said that he found it out on the Pedregal. But I know that wasn't true."

She paused and looked about her. Waiting, Rennert knew, for a question.

61

"How did you know it wasn't true?" he asked.

"Because I saw him pick it up out of a gully that the rain had washed along the wall north of the coach house. He was walking along the edge of this gully and looking down into it. Then I saw him stoop and pick something up. When he was showing it to Marta I went up to see what it was. Of course, after he said that he had found it in the Pedregal, I couldn't very well contradict him. I did act very knowing, though, to show him that he wasn't deceiving me."

"What was it like, Monica?" Lucy asked with increasing interest.

"Well, I've never seen a coin exactly like it. It wasn't Mexican, I'm sure. It was square, about the size of a five-centavo piece, and had little knobs at the top and bottom. It had lain in the ground so long that you couldn't tell much about it. There were letters, though, in some foreign language and a date. I told John—Mr. Biggerstaff—about it. I thought he might know what kind of coin it was or might look it up in the National Library in Mexico City, but he was getting ready to go on his trip, so he didn't pay much attention."

"On his last trip, to the border?"

"Yes. It was about a week ago. If you want to see the coin, Señor Echave still has it."

"He has?"

"Yes, it's on a string about his neck. At least that's what Marta told me. If you find buried gold and carry a piece of it close to your heart, it'll bring you good luck, you know."

The tattoo of Lucy's cane was increasing in tempo.

"Mr. Rennert," she said, "all this talk is getting you nowhere, and I know that you're a busy man. The answer to the problem of Mr. Voice's murder lies, I am sure, not with us, but with a group of archaeologists who are living upstairs. They are the Teague Museum party, and it was in their shipment that you found the skeleton. I may as well tell you that they are here in the house against my wishes. I know them only slightly."

"But, Lucy," Monica said, "you know John Biggerstaff."

"On the contrary, Monica, I do not know him at all. He seems a nice enough, well-mannered young man, but I doubt very much that he is what he pretends to be."

Monica's laugh rattled. "It's Lucy who's being imaginative now, Mr. Rennert. She thinks that John is a suspicious character because of his accent."

"His accent?" Rennert was interested.

"Yes," Lucy broke in firmly. "Mr. Biggerstaff has called on me several times. Last Easter he brought me a present of some lilies. I endeavored to draw him into conversation about his background. He seemed very reticent about this, although he assured me that he was born and raised in the South, that his ancestors had fought in the Civil War. When I questioned him more closely, however, I found that he either could not or would not give me a single bit of specific information. He spoke in a very pronounced Southern accent. Too pronounced to be real. I am sure that he has affected it, for what reason I can't imagine. I had heard him talking to his companions in an altogether different voice. Therefore I have my doubts about him."

She was silent for a moment, her lips compressed. She seemed to be deliberating the advisability of continuing on this subject. Abruptly she changed.

"The other young man, Weikel I think his name is, is most uncouth. He has no breeding at all. My few experiences with him have been most unpleasant. He used to throw stones at the songbirds about the house, then leave them lying on the ground wounded. I soon put a stop to that. Then this spring he began putting his traps downstairs, in the halls and in the kitchen. He was very insolent to Marta when she told him not to do it."

Rennert asked curiously, "His traps?"

"Yes, mousetraps. He complained of being bothered with mice in his room. He felt at liberty to go over the entire house, laying traps. I caught him at it once." Lucy's lips set grimly. "Since then I have not had occasion to speak to him."

She seemed to drift away into thought again, then turned to him in quick decision. "Mr. Rennert, it is your mission here in Mexico to clear up this mystery, is it not?"

"Yes, Miss Faudree. Mr. Roark here is assisting me."

"As you can see, it is a matter of honor for me to aid you in every way possible, since Professor Voice was a guest in our home at the time of his death. But the news is so unexpected that I can think of no solution at the moment. Perhaps tomorrow I shall be of more help. In the meantime you will, of course, honor us by accepting our hospitality during your stay in Mexico."

Rennert was frankly surprised. "But, Miss Faudree, that would be too much of an imposition. I can obtain quite comfortable accommodations at the San Angel Inn."

She raised a hand in an imperative gesture. "Mr. Rennert, the Faudrees have always been famed for their hospitality. I should feel that I had failed our tradition if I allowed you to stay in a common inn while you are doing us a service. Let us consider the matter settled. I am only sorry that we can offer you no more in the way of entertainment. Since my father's death we have lived very quietly here. I trust, though, that the spirit of hospitality has remained unimpaired."

"Thank you, then, Miss Faudree. I shall be delighted to avail myself of your invitation."

"Would you like to be shown to your room now?"

"At any time. Would you mind if Mr. Roark took me about the grounds before it gets too dark?"

"Not at all. You are to make yourselves perfectly at home."

"And you spoke of Mr. Voice's belongings. Would it be convenient for me to look them over?"

"Certainly. They are in the coach house. Monica, get my keys, will you?"

"Yes, Lucy." Monica got to her feet with alacrity and stuffed the handkerchief into a pocket. "Oh, Mr. Rennert, we are so glad that you're staying with us. I shall be so interested in watching you work. Will—"

"Mr. Rennert is in a hurry, Monica," Lucy said. "Didn't you hear him say he wanted to look around before it gets dark?"

"Yes, of course." Monica hurried out.

"Dinner will be at seven," Lucy said when the sound of the shoes had died away across the hall. "Will you join us, Mr. Roark?"

The young man hesitated. "I'm sorry, but I have an engagement in Mexico City."

"That's too bad. Some other time then."

Rennert had been considering his next question. "Miss Faudree, there's one more favor I'm going to ask of you. Might I examine the letters that Professor Voice was working on?"

Her frown was very slight and almost instantly gone. "Why of course. They're merely old family correspondence, but you are welcome to see them. I have them in my room. I will give them to you at dinner."

"Thank you."

Lucy looked about the room. Her laugh was too light and brittle to be the product of anything except nervous tension.

"There is something for which I must apologize, Mr. Rennert. Your visit has coincided with the failure of the lights. There has been some accident on the line, I suppose, and the electricity is turned off. It may be impossible to have it repaired before tomorrow. Marta will leave candles in your room."

"Don't worry, Miss Faudree. I shall fare very well." So that explained the unsatisfactory illumination of the candles while an electric lamp and wall brackets were unlit. This contingency would hamper his work irritatingly. One other night, down in Taxco, he had had to depend on wax tapers as he felt his way cautiously through a maze not unlike this. . . .

Monica returned and handed Lucy a number of old-fashioned keys on a thin blue ribbon.

Lucy disentangled the knot. "This is the key to the storeroom in the loft of the coach house. There are stairs going up the north side. You will find Mr. Voice's things there."

"By the way," Rennert said as he took the key, "were any of his possessions missing when they were put away?"

"I don't think so. Marta carried them out. You may ask her if you wish. If you will ring for her, Monica, she can show Mr. Rennert to his room."

One of Monica's hands rose to pat at her hair. "Oh, I will take them up, Lucy. I am going up anyway. I wouldn't think of troubling Marta. Just come this way, Mr. Rennert and Mr. Roark." She shepherded them toward the door.

In the hall she fell into step between them and said as they started up the stairs:

"Really, Mr. Rennert, you are my guest, you know. Your room belongs to me, not to Lucy."

"I trust you don't begrudge me the welcome she extended?"

"Not at all. I should have asked you if she hadn't." On the landing she saw his gaze go to the small vestibule at the foot of the rear stairs. "Those are the back stairs," she explained. "The archaeologists use them to go to their work. It's very convenient. That door on the right is to Lucy's room, the other to the kitchen."

She paused at the head of the stairs and indicated the door behind them and to their right. "There's my room. Those two doors at the end of the hall go to Cornell's apartment upstairs and to the bath. Then across the hall is where Mr. Biggerstaff, Mr. Weikel and Dr. Fogarty live." She led the way to the left of the stair well. "This is your room, Mr. Rennert."

Large and high-ceilinged as the chamber was, the four-poster bed against the west wall gave it a crowded effect. One scarcely noticed the other furniture—a tall wardrobe with a double mirror set in the doors, a secretary, old comfortable-looking chairs—before the magnificence of the bed.

"I do hope you will like it here, Mr. Rennert." Monica had the handkerchief out and was pulling at it again. "It's the room where Mr. Voice stayed. Do you mind that?"

"Not at all."

"I didn't think you'd be—well, squeamish. You have a good view of the Pedregal from here too."

Roark had already walked over to the south window and was staring out.

They joined him.

The clouds had hidden the sun entirely now, and the place looked more desolate than ever, with its surface contours smoothed by the premature twilight. Sixty feet or so from the rear of the house the lava ended in a jagged wall twice the height of a man's head. From what seemed a black, flat plain beyond three cacti stood out like obscene symbols of a phallic cult. . . .

Monica said suddenly, "Mr. Rennert, I want to ask you something."

"Yes?" His eyes and thoughts had been on those cacti, in alignment with this window so straight that it might have been premeditated.

"It's about that letter which was supposed to have come from Mr. Voice. Is it really important?"

"It might have been very important, Miss Faudree."

"How?"

"Each typewriter gives an individual writing which is easily identifiable. If, as I think, that letter was written by the murderer of Professor Voice, I might have located the machine on which it was made."

Monica was breathless. "Oh, I didn't know that. Will you promise not to tell Lucy if I give you that letter?"

10
DRINK

AT THIS RATE, Rennert thought, it would become a habit to stare at Monica.

"Then you have the letter?" he asked.

She seemed uneasy under the gaze of the two men, fidgeting, while a spot of color appeared on either cheek. "Yes."

"In that case you may rely upon my promise."

"I can't explain just why I don't want Lucy to know about it, but you know how these things are, Mr. Rennert."

Rennert didn't know what she meant, but said: "Of course. Would it be convenient for you to let me have it now?"

The crimson of her cheeks was more pronounced. "I can't give it to you right now, Mr. Rennert. It'll take a little time. But I'll give it to you. I promise."

Rennert was curious. "You don't have it in the house?"

"Oh yes, it's in the house. In my room. But really I can't give it to you now. You see," she finished in a kind of desperation, "I have to find it first."

"You'll look for it right away?"

"Oh yes, as soon as I have a little time."

"Very well. Mr. Roark and I have to go upstairs for a few minutes. Then we want to look over the grounds. Perhaps you will have located it by that time and can give it to me at dinner?"

"I'll try, Mr. Rennert. You're going up to see John?"

"Yes. The doctor has given me the responsibility of seeing that he goes to bed and gets a rest. It's about time I attended to my duties."

"You don't need to worry about him at all, Mr. Rennert. John will want *me* to take care of him, I know. I was going back up there myself."

"Of course. But I promised the doctor—"

"All right then." Her tone was a trifle piqued. "We can go up together. But you will see that John will want *me* at his bedside."

As they went down the hall she said:

"John is just the same as a nephew to me, Mr. Rennert. He's such a dear boy, so kind and considerate. You mustn't pay any attention to what Lucy said about him. She's only jealous because he prefers me to her."

She paused at the door to the third flight of stairs. Her smile was arch. "Perhaps we'd better knock. You know these young people, Mr. Rennert. And I suppose it's no secret to you by this time that John *may* be—I only say *may* be, understand—a real nephew to me one of these days."

Cornell opened the door just then. Rennert thought that there was a shade of annoyance on her face as she saw Monica. She smiled, however, and led them upstairs.

"If an appetite's any indication," she said, "our patient is on the road to recovery."

They found Biggerstaff sunk deep in a chair, a tray upon his lap. He was finishing a sandwich.

"Hello!" he greeted, his mouth full. "Time's not up yet, is it, Mr. Rennert?"

"It is."

Monica had brushed past Rennert and was bending over Biggerstaff, her hands fluttering about the bandage.

"My dear boy, you must go to bed immediately! I can't have you running any risks with that poor head of yours. Why, there's no telling what you might do to your brain. You must let me take you downstairs at once. I'll sit with you till you fall asleep."

Biggerstaff shoved the tray onto a table, got up and said determinedly:

"Now see here, Monica. I've told you I'm all right. There's nothing to get bothered about. And I have something to say to Mr. Rennert and Mr. Roark. In private. Understand?"

He looked very small and pugnacious, standing there in front of her.

She quickly inserted a hand in the crook of his elbow and said to the others:

"That's typical of John. Not wanting to cause me any trouble."

Biggerstaff pulled himself free. His eyes twinkled as he held up his bandaged arm. "What I want, Monica, is somebody to help me out of my underwear." And, in a note of triumph, as Monica raised her handkerchief to her mouth and coughed, "Shall we go downstairs, gentlemen?"

As the three men walked toward the stairs he turned to Cornell, standing alone on one side of the room. "Good night, dear."

"Good night."

On the second floor Biggerstaff stopped. "Do you mind if I tell Dr. Fogarty about my job? It'll only take a moment."

He was off down the hall. He knocked on the far door on the right-hand side, but there was no response. He started back and paused by the middle door. "I'll tell Karl Weikel too, I guess."

He rapped on the panel.

The door opened, and he said cheerfully, "Hello, Karl. How are you?"

A "Hello" came in a decidedly guttural voice. "When'd you get back?"

"This afternoon. Karl, I got some news. From the museum."

The hallway was rather dark, and Rennert had to shift his position before he had a view of the man who stood in the door. He was dressed in work clothes—corduroy trousers and boots. He was about Biggerstaff's age and height, but a great deal broader and heavier. His head was large and covered with a shock of uncombed chalky hair. Rennert wondered how much the fellow's tan and the poor light accounted for the sullen, forbidding cast of his coarse features, with the Semitic nose and thick lips.

He said, "I suppose you got the job?"

"Yes, I start to work September first." Biggerstaff seemed confused when the other said nothing. "I—I thought I'd tell you about it."

"You don't think it's anything to boast about, do you?" Weikel demanded unpleasantly.

"Why no, Karl. I'm not boasting."

"The hell you aren't. What're you telling me about it for, then?"

"I thought you might like to know."

"I know you got the job. That's enough."

"But, Karl, I didn't . . ." Biggerstaff was getting angry.

Weikel laughed loudly. "You didn't tell 'em who you are? Listen, don't hand me that stuff—" he paused and underscored the syllables—"*Biggerstaff!*"

He turned and slammed the door.

Biggerstaff didn't look at Rennert and Roark as he came down the hall and opened the door of his room. "Come in," he said unsteadily.

The room was of approximately the same size as Rennert's. One corner had been partitioned off into a clothes closet. There were two chairs, a chiffonier and a brass bed, all inexpensive factory-made products. A small deal table stood by the window.

Biggerstaff moved toward the bed. One side of his face was screwed up, and he was rubbing his thumb over his forehead above the eyebrows.

"Let's get those clothes off," Rennert said sternly. "You can talk in the meantime."

"Oh, I think I can manage them all right. I just said what I did on account of Monica. She means all right, but she's rather a trial at times. Cornell and I never have a chance to be together as long as we stay here. We usually have to go for a walk. But what I wanted to tell you was about those letters that came to Mr. Voice."

As he spoke he was endeavoring to wriggle out of his coat.

Rennert stepped up to him and helped him slide the bandaged hand through the sleeve. Roark took the coat and carried it to the closet.

"Thanks." Biggerstaff's fingers jerked at his tie and managed to get it unfastened.

"Cornell and I were talking about those letters." He sank onto the bed and began to unlace his shoes. "You remember I said that if you really thought they had any connection with his murder I'd tell you who I thought wrote them. It was only a suspicion, and it seemed like it'd be disloyal if I tried to throw suspicion on an associate of mine. But Cornell thinks differently. She says that all of us have got to help you by giving you all the information we can. So here goes. I don't give a damn now if you *do* know it. I was sure—and I *am* sure that Karl Weikel wrote those letters."

He straightened suddenly, his eyes closed. His lips were white. "Just the blood running to my head," he said as he forced a weak smile.

Rennert gestured to Roark, who bent down and pulled off the shoe on which Biggerstaff had been working.

When that was done he gently but firmly forced Biggerstaff down until his head rested against the pillow. "Take it easy, son. Take it easy."

Biggerstaff went on talking, jerkily:

"Karl's never been a particular friend of mine, though I've known him for a long time. Since he's a member of our party, though, I'd like to keep him out of trouble if I can. I still don't think he had anything to do with a murder, but I do think he wrote those letters."

"I suppose you have reasons for thinking that?" Rennert said quietly. He was unbuttoning Biggerstaff's shirt while Roark pulled off his trousers. The young man made no resistance.

"It's only a suspicion," he talked on. "But here's what I've got to go on. Weikel and Mr. Voice never got on together. They had trouble back in the university. I know that Karl disliked Voice and was always threatening to get even with him. I remember borrowing a magazine from Karl this winter sometime. There was a story in it about some bandits who kidnapped an American and held him for ransom out in the mountains. When his friends wouldn't pay the money they—well, they cut him up pretty badly and sent him into town. He had to walk after the soles of his feet had been flayed. Well, I know that Karl read that story. And when I saw the letters that Voice got, I remembered that the letters were worded about the same as those in the story. I'll tell you what I did. I was in Karl's room one day and saw that magazine in a stack of others. I looked at it—and sure enough, they were almost identically the same. Even to the three cacti. That was the title of the story. Those three back of the house may have reminded him of it. Now that's all I know, and I hope you won't think from that that Karl *did* kill Voice. But—but Cornell wanted me to tell you."

He finished breathlessly and lay very still, his eyes closed.

Roark had found a pair of pajamas and was pulling the trousers over Biggerstaff's legs. With his knife Rennert slit the strap of the undershirt and drew it off. He was rather concerned about the young fellow's condition and wanted to avoid any disturbance of the bandage.

"You needn't worry, Biggerstaff. I promise you I won't jump to any conclusions about Weikel. We'll talk it over tomorrow."

"There's one thing more, Mr. Rennert."

"What's that?"

"About two months ago I took another shipment of stuff to the border. Pottery. When they unpacked it at the museum there were forgeries in it."

Rennert's fingers stopped on the top button of the pajama coat. "Were they ever accounted for?"

"No. The pottery was genuine when it was packed. I know because I helped. Dr. Fogarty decided it must have been done at the railway station or on the train. I couldn't stay in the baggage car all the time," he concluded defensively.

"Of course not," Rennert agreed. "Forget about it for the present. Where's that sedative the doctor gave you?"

"In my coat pocket," Biggerstaff said as he slipped between the sheets.

Rennert found the small oblong box while Roark procured a glass of water from the bathroom. He dissolved two of the tablets and handed the tumbler to Biggerstaff.

The latter propped himself up on an elbow and grinned in embarrassment as he stared into the colorless liquid. "I feel like a damned sissy being taken care of this way, but my head *does* hurt a little, I'll admit."

Rennert came back from the window, which he had opened several inches. "Drink that, and you'll be all right. We'll see you in the morning."

"All right. Good night."

"Good night."

He had the glass at his lips as they went out.

11
FIST

KARL WEIKEL was crossing the hall toward the stairs as they came out. He gave them a bold, direct stare but did not pause or make any gesture of greeting.

Rennert waited until the rear door had slammed shut, then beckoned Roark to follow him. He opened the door of Weikel's room, and they went in.

The arrangement of these quarters was identical with that of Biggerstaff's, save that there was a single window instead of two. The air was bad, charged with a disagreeably medicinal odor.

Rennert smiled as he saw Roark regarding him questioningly. "My customs training," he explained. "I can't keep away from people's personal belongings. They never fail to answer questions."

He began a swift, methodical examination of the room.

In the space which had been partitioned off as a closet he found a pair of half-soled shoes, a gray-and-black striped suit, much worn, and a raincoat; on the ledge above, a felt hat, an imitation-leather suitcase, empty, and, pushed back on one end, four mouse-traps. One of these he brought down.

It was a cheap contraption, such as might be bought in any store, and gave no evidence of recent usage. Its prongs were stained reddish brown with what looked like rust, but wasn't.

Roark, who had been standing in the center of the room watching him, laughed slightly and said:

"As your slow-witted Watson, is it my cue to ask what's the meaning of that thing?"

Rennert shook his head slowly. "Please don't. I'd find it difficult to hide the fact that I haven't the faintest idea. It may be that
the young man simply doesn't like mice."

He put the trap back into place and turned to the table which
stood to one side of the window.

On its surface were disorderly stacks of papers, an old pipe,
and a can of cheap tobacco, a few desiccated bones. In the center
lay a dozen or more fragments of pottery, some glued together,
others single. On each of them had been pasted a small label with
a number and a name printed in ink.

Rennert sank into the chair and drew from his pocket the two
threatening letters which had been sent to Professor Voice. One
by one he picked up the shards and compared the printing with
that on the letters.

He looked up to meet the gaze of Roark, who was standing at
his shoulder. "Well, Watson, what's the verdict?"

"I'd say that Weikel was our letter writer," Roark said without
hesitation.

Rennert nodded. "Unfortunately printing isn't as easily identified as handwriting. But I shouldn't be surprised if an expert could
find something in the way of proof here. The ink perhaps. At any
rate, we can see."

He found a discarded newspaper, selected several of the pottery fragments and wrapped them up.

"Looks bad for Weikel, doesn't it?" Roark commented. "After
what Biggerstaff told us about him."

Rennert was silent for a moment.

"You went to college, didn't you?" he asked suddenly.

"Yes."

"And doubtless considered yourself so important that you
thought some of your professors spent all their time thinking up
ways to discriminate against you. If you didn't get a high grade in
some course, it wasn't because you didn't deserve it, but because
of favoritism."

"Yes, I suppose that's true."

"I know it was in my case. It's the natural undergraduate attitude. Silly, but understandable. Well, I haven't told you yet that I

wired a friend of mine who's teaching at Southwestern University for information about these archaeologists. Particularly their relations with Voice. Here's his reply."

He took a telegram from his pocket and handed it to Roark. "Wordy, but he wasn't paying for it."

He watched the other's face as he read:

> DR. FOGARTY HIGHLY RESPECTED MEMBER OF FACULTY HERE BEFORE RESIGNATION TO GO TO TEAGUE MUSEUM STOP JOHN BIGGERSTAFF EXCELLENT RECORD SCHOLASTIC AND PERSONAL STOP KNOW OF NO CONNECTION WITH VOICE STOP KARL WEIKEL EXCELLENT RECORD SOME SUBJECTS POOR IN OTHERS STOP FREQUENTLY IN TROUBLE WITH AUTHORITIES ACCOUNT RADICAL AGITATION STOP WAS REFUSED DEGREE LAST SPRING BECAUSE HE STRUCK VOICE IN LATTER'S OFFICE STOP ACCUSED VOICE LOWERING HISTORY GRADE TO KEEP HIM OUT PHI BETA KAPPA STOP MADE THREATS

Roark gave vent to a low whistle as he folded the telegram and handed it back to Rennert. "Phi Beta Kappa! Hmmm. Well, I suppose it won't be the first time there's been scandal in the order."

Rennert said, "Is it because I've been out of the halls of learning so long that I find it hard to take undergraduate grudges seriously? Election to an honor society is a big thing at the time, but it diminishes in retrospect. And when it comes to murder! I'll swear, Roark, I can't see it!"

"I admit it sounds a bit preposterous. But the Phi Beta Kappa election may have been only one factor."

Rennert nodded. "True." He glanced at the window and got up. "We'd better hurry if we're going to look over the grounds before dark."

Back in his own room Rennert deposited the bundle of pottery in a drawer of the wardrobe.

"Exhibit B, I suppose," Roark commented. "The letters are A."

"You forget the bullet from Voice's skull. That's A."

"Oh yes." Roark tapped a cigarette on the back of his hand. "It's from a revolver of the same caliber as the one you got from Cornell, isn't it?"

"Yes." Rennert's finger explored the right-hand vest pocket in which it reposed, securely sealed in a small envelope.

"You're going to compare the bullets?"

"I'll have a ballistics expert do it."

Roark cupped his hands over a match. "You're not expecting that they'll be the same, are you?"

"I think it's improbable that they are."

The gray-blue eyes looked squarely into Rennert's. "See here, Rennert, I haven't got the interest in this business the old man has. I don't give a whoop in hell about the Teague influence. But I don't want to see Cornell drawn into this. You can take my word for it that she's as straight a girl as ever lived. I knew her a long time ago. She won't have changed."

"My interest in her gun doesn't necessarily imply any suspicion of her, Roark. Remember that Biggerstaff used that gun. Others may have. It's only common sense to have its bullets examined."

"Oh sure, I know." Roark seemed mollified. "I just thought I'd make it clear about Cornell." He glanced at his watch. "Did you want me to stay out here for dinner? I could break that date if necessary."

"By no means. All I want to do right now is get acquainted with these people. For that reason I'm glad of the invitation to stay in the house."

"That was rather a surprise. I didn't know how Lucy would receive you. As long as she thinks you're safeguarding the family honor, she'll turn the place over to you. By the way, the chauffeur's waiting out in front. He can get your bags for you. Where are they?"

"I travel light. One gladstone. It's at the San Angel Inn. I had it sent out from the airport."

"Good. You can call the hotel from here and cancel your reservation."

"Didn't I understand both you and Biggerstaff to say that the phone wasn't in order?"

Roark frowned. "I'd forgotten that."

"I'll make sure."

Rennert went into the hall, where the telephone stood on a low table between the stairs and his room. He consulted the directory and dialed the number of the inn.

While he waited for a response the door of Cornell's apartment opened and Monica Faudree came out.

Evidently the failing light prevented her from seeing them, for she started directly across to Biggerstaff's room.

Rennert called, "Oh, Miss Faudree, I wouldn't go in there if I were you. Biggerstaff's asleep."

She wheeled about, momentarily disconcerted, and advanced a few steps in his direction. "I was just going in to sit beside him until I was sure he was asleep. I'm sure my presence would soothe him. I've been talking to Cornell about how dangerous these head injuries can be sometimes. I want to be sure he's resting."

"He was sleeping soundly when we left him," Rennert prevaricated. "You might wake him up if you went in. That would be unwise, I know."

Her chin rose slightly. "Mr. Rennert, I know more about what John needs than you do. I'll take my knitting in, and if he's asleep I'll just sit there until dinnertime." She turned and marched in the direction of her room.

Rennert let the receiver fall.

"No answer?" Roark said sharply.

"The line's dead."

The other cleared his throat nervously. "Strange that the lights and the telephone should both be out of commission. There hasn't been any storm to break the wires."

Rennert stared thoughtfully down the hall, where the darkness was thickening so swiftly.

"The strange thing," he said, "is the coincidence which Lucy mentioned. With my visit."

Both of them were silent as Monica came out of her room, a knitted bag swinging on her arm. She paused. "Oh, you wanted to use the phone, didn't you? I'm so sorry. You see—" she faltered— "something's wrong with it. I don't know what. Was it anything important?"

"No, nothing important. Have the telephone and lights been out of order long?"

"Only today." She was already headed toward Biggerstaff's room again.

They saw her turn the knob quietly and go in. Just as the door closed they had a glimpse of her face. She was smiling.

Roark said, "Damn! Well, no matter. The chauffeur will attend to it. While he's gone I can introduce you to Fogarty, if he's at the excavations. What do you want me to tell him about you?"

"Merely explain that I'm from the United States customs. Leave the rest to me."

Their sleeves touched as they went down the narrow flight of stairs to the vestibule.

"I wonder," Roark said, "what Weikel meant by his remark to Biggerstaff about that museum job? About telling who he was?"

Rennert shook his head. "I've been wondering that myself."

"He seems all right. And it looks as if Cornell were in love with him, doesn't it?"

"From what I've observed, yes."

"I don't think she'd make a mistake," Roark said slowly as he opened the door.

Outside, they stood for a moment looking at the scene.

The ground between them and the lava was covered to about half its extent by thick, lush grass. This ended abruptly upon an expanse of bare, dark soil cut by gullies.

On their left were the remains of a cedar tree, shattered by lightning at some distant time. On their right was the coach house, a huge wooden structure modeled after the residence.

At the base of the cliff an iron gate had been set in a narrow opening some five feet high. In a semicircle about this were mounds of debris, cemented by time and the weather to the semblance of prehistoric truncated pyramids.

On one of these a man was standing. He was tall, well over six feet, with bunched shoulders and long arms. His head was bare, and he was staring fixedly out over the lava.

As the two of them watched he raised his right hand with a jerky movement and, like an angry child, shook his fist in the direction of the swirling rain clouds which were blanketing Mount Ajusco.

"Dr. Fogarty," Roark whispered.

12
CLAY

AT THE SOUND of their feet on the loose stones the man turned to survey them, his heavy brows drawn into a frown.

He had a long, lined face with rugged features tanned to a chrome-leather hue. In contrast his candid gray-blue eyes seemed extraordinarily light.

"Hullo!" His gruffness made the words sound like a challenge.

"I don't know that you remember me, Dr. Fogarty." Roark stepped up. "I'm Delaney Roark, from the United States Embassy."

"Oh yes, yes." Fogarty shook hands perfunctorily.

"And this is Mr. Rennert, of the United States Customs Service."

The archaeologist's hand took Rennert's briefly, then went to lodge in the hip pocket of his dust-streaked corduroy trousers. There was only passing interest in his glance.

"It's enough to try Job's own patience!" He reverted to his own preoccupation.

Roark passed a palm back from the even part of his hair. "What's wrong, Doctor?"

"Wrong?" Fogarty's heavy shoes grated on the gravel. He jerked the hand from his pocket and pointed to the sky over the lava. It was a large hand, calloused, and tufted on the back with thick hairs powdered by dust.

"The rain!" he said. "Don't you see it? It comes every day now. We're having to postpone work until next season. It's maddening."

82

"But this is the regular time for the summer rains to begin, Doctor." Rennert tried to be conciliating. "Surely you must have been expecting them?"

"Expecting them? Yes. But, man, look what they're interrupting. That's what I wasn't expecting. Look!" He squatted on the ground and gestured toward a burlap bag spread there. On it were a dozen or so broken pieces of pottery, reddish brown in color, and a smaller object of terra cotta in the shape of a human body.

"Molded!" Fogarty exclaimed. "Molded, I'm positive! Do you realize what that means? Do you? In an Archaic site?"

He looked somewhat like a tortoise, old and no longer agile, sitting there on his heels and craning his head around to look up into their faces. Suddenly his chapped lips broke into a good-natured smile.

"Sorry!" he chuckled. "Of course you don't realize. I was forgetting myself. I was excited. See this figurine. It's made on a mold, one of a pattern."

He held it out with no seeming intention of relinquishing his grasp on it. When Rennert took it from his hand with sudden interest, he frowned and warned quickly, "Be careful with it, please."

He got to his feet, his surprise at Rennert's minute examination of the piece apparent.

"This site, gentlemen, belongs to what we call the Archaic period, the earliest known in Mexico. Prior to the Toltec and the Aztec. Of the same date, we've thought, as that at Copilco, which Professor Gamio studied. But all true Archaic pottery is modeled by hand, not molded. Each piece made separately. At least that has been the consensus of opinion for years. Now, what's the answer? Is this a post-Archaic site? No, I'm sure it's not. The pottery we've found, the skeletons, all tell the same story. Gentlemen, why not the alternative theory? That we have come to a transitional site—between the true Archaic and what we call so vaguely the Toltec? But—mark this—it lies under the same lava as the undoubtedly true Archaic site at Copilco. You see what that means? It places these people at a much more advanced state of culture than we had thought. Therefore it extends their horizon backward—who knows how many centuries? Man may have come to the Valley of Mexico much, much earlier than we have believed. The importance of this find may be—why, it may be epochal!"

Rennert's fingers still held the little piece of ancient clay. He was staring down at it so intently that he was oblivious of Fogarty's expectant glance.

It was a grotesque caricature of a naked human being, perhaps an inch and a half high. The head was broad and tapered to a small, angular chin. The face was blank and moronlike, with features represented by mere scratches in the clay. Contrasting with this was the mouth, wherein the malignancy of the thing resided. The lips were huge and blubbery, and were set in an evil, mocking snicker. The body might have been the work of an idle child, save for the buttocks, which were realistically fashioned but so disproportionate that they made the whole seem some figment of a feverish imagination.

"Almost eight months we have worked here!" Fogarty was going on, with Roark for an audience. "At first we found nothing. We tunneled further and further back under the lava and found nothing. It was discouraging, I can tell you. Then we began to come across some pottery and figurines. All of them modeled by hand, as was to be expected. Then for weeks work was stopped on account of lack of funds. We started again—and found nothing. And now, when we've come to what is undoubtedly the beginning of a large site, with buildings, mind you, buildings—the rains stop us. Gentlemen—" his voice vibrated with intensity—"I'd almost be willing to see all the crops in the Valley die if I could have one more month of work!"

"You have my sympathy, Doctor," Rennert said, "but three months isn't so long to wait."

Fogarty's head began to go to and fro mechanically.

"This must be my last season," he said. "I'm growing too old for such active work. I must turn it over to younger, more active men."

There was a moment of silence.

Rennert said, "I'm interested in this figurine, Doctor. May I ask if it is unusual? I'm not referring to the manner of manufacture, of course, but to the design. I'm under the impression that I have seen many like it in museums here in Mexico."

Dr. Fogarty, suddenly mindful of the artifact, took it from Rennert's hand and slipped it into a pocket.

"Oh yes," he said, "they're very common. Archaeologists dig 'em up by the hundreds. You'll find many similar to this one."

"I have always been fascinated—and a little repelled—by the grotesqueness of some of them. This one for example."

"Yes." There was a good-natured twinkle in the archaeologist's eyes as he looked at Rennert. "You can see that the Mexican flair for caricature is deep-rooted. Some of these terra-cotta pieces are startlingly lifelike. Others are, as you say, grotesque. The worker would seize on some prominent feature of one of his neighbors and distort it out of all proportion. Some of them, too, are doubtless images of dwarfs and freaks. Even in historic times these were looked on with a little awe. Montezuma had a menagerie of them."

He continued to regard Rennert. "You say you're with the U. S. Customs Service?"

"Yes, stationed at Laredo."

"At Laredo, huh? We send a lot of stuff through there."

"So I know, Doctor. It is in connection with your shipments that I'm here."

"It is? Anything wrong?"

"The last shipment of skeletons which Mr. Biggerstaff was taking up was damaged in a wreck of the Mexican National."

"Damaged! Oh, my God!" In his agitation Fogarty shoved a hand through his thinning gray hair. "This is the last straw! Where's Biggerstaff? Why didn't he make a report to me?"

"Mr. Biggerstaff was injured. I brought him down with me by plane. He's in his room now."

There was genuine concern on the archaeologist's face. "Is the boy seriously hurt?"

"Not seriously. He won't be able to work for a few weeks, however."

"In his room, you say? I'll go see him."

"We've given him a sedative by the doctor's orders. He's not to be disturbed until morning."

"Oh! But what became of the skeletons?"

"They were sent on to the museum in San Antonio. I believe that the damage can be repaired very easily. I am down here to make a few inquiries about that shipment."

"Inquiries?" Fogarty shot at him.

Rennert knew it wasn't his fancy; that the man's eyes had lost their good humor and grown suddenly wary and sharp.

"To begin with, Doctor, I'd like to have the history of those skeletons from the moment they were uncovered under the lava to the time they were sent to the railway station."

Fogarty answered readily enough: "They were found about two weeks ago. I have the exact date in my notes. My assistant, Karl Weikel, made the actual discovery. Biggerstaff and I helped get them out. They were cleaned and reinforced for shipping. That took some time, as they were in a rather bad condition. Then they were packed in plaster casts and boxed—"

"When was that done? And where?"

"Last week. All the work on 'em was done in the coach house yonder. We use it as a laboratory."

"The skeletons remained there from the time they were dug up until Biggerstaff took them away?"

"Yes."

"Guarded?"

"Well, not exactly guarded. But they were safe enough. The doors to the old stables were padlocked. And Marta, the family servant, sleeps in a room next to them. Besides, there's not much danger of any prowlers about here. The natives shun the vicinity of the Pedregal at night. It's a haunted spot, they think."

"Mr. Biggerstaff takes these shipments of yours to the border frequently?"

"This is the second time. He took some pottery about two months ago."

"I understand there was some trouble about it."

THE CASE OF THE UNCONQUERED SISTERS

Fogarty's frown and pursed lips evidenced his perturbation.

"Yes," he said, as if weighing his words with extreme care. "There was. Almost half of it consisted of forgeries."

"Did you learn who was responsible?"

"No. It wasn't discovered until the stuff got to the museum in San Antonio. They were very good imitations, but they wouldn't have fooled an expert for a moment. I decided that a band of expert forgers must be at work and that the substitution must have been made at the station."

"You're sure it couldn't have been made here on the grounds?"

"I don't see how."

"Do you employ workmen?"

"No. We hired some natives at the start, to get the tunnel driven under the lava. But this spring my two assistants and I have done all the work. It cuts down the expense."

"This last shipment bore the stamp of the Mexican Department of Archaeology. It was signed by one of their inspectors, Diego Echave. What was the extent of his examination of it?"

Fogarty cleared his throat noisily.

"Echave examines all our finds," he said with a trace of peremptoriness. "He visits the excavations daily and takes out the government's share. Certainly he examined those skeletons."

"And the previous shipment as well?"

"Yes. He would have detected it at once if there'd been any forgeries when the cases left here."

"You say he visits your excavations daily. Has he been out today?"

Fogarty frowned and kicked at a stone. "Why no, he hasn't."

"But you're expecting him?"

"Well . . . I don't know. I don't really think so. We haven't been finding a great deal lately."

"If he comes, I wonder if you would have him see me. I'm staying with the Faudrees for the present."

Fogarty stared at him for a moment. "See here, Mr. Rennert, are you investigating those pottery forgeries too?"

"Yes."

"It's a rather late date to be doing that. I'm afraid I haven't any more information to give you. The specimens were genuine when they left here. Now if you gentlemen will pardon me . . . ? I'm very busy right now. I must remove these specimens to the coach house before the rain starts."

As he bent over, Rennert signaled to Roark. "Let us help you, Doctor. I don't think you can carry all that by yourself."

"No, no, don't bother." Fogarty made a motion of the hand as if to brush them away. "I can carry 'em. They're very fragile."

With an attempt at casualness which didn't, Rennert felt, deceive the archaeologist, he and Roark knelt down and assisted him to pick up the dusty fragments of clay.

Fogarty said nothing, but ill-concealed vexation darkened his face as they straightened up and walked toward the coach house.

This seemed to be divided into halves. On the left two large sliding doors were pushed back to reveal the dim interior of what had been the stables. Windows indicated that a lower and upper room occupied the right section.

Fogarty tramped a few feet ahead of them until he arrived in front of the doors. Here he turned. "It's rather dirty inside, gentlemen. Thank you very much. Just put the things down on the ground."

But Rennert had already stepped inside.

The removal of the stalls had left a great deal of space. The floor was of brick, overlaid by a thick layer of dust. There were trestle tables ranged along the walls, most of them piled high with odd-shaped stones and pottery. In the corners were packing cases, sacks, spades, shovels and picks.

Two men who had been leaning against one of the tables straightened as they entered.

Fogarty followed Rennert in and stood for a moment as if uncertain of his next move. Finally he dumped down the pottery which he had been carrying (with great disregard, Rennert observed, for the fragility of which he had warned) and said, "Lay the things any place."

When they had obeyed there was another strained pause.

Fogarty slapped at his sleeve and sent a little cloud of dust into the still air.

"Hello, Echave," he said gruffly. "Didn't know you were here. This is Mr. Roark. And Mr. Rennert."

He added very distinctly, as the man came forward, "Mr. Rennert is from the United States Customs Service."

13
LOFT

"THE UNITED STATES CUSTOMS SERVICE."

The words were an echo, soft and full-voweled, of Fogarty's consonantal ones.

The Mexican hesitated for an almost imperceptible instant, then held out a manicured hand. "It is a pleasure, Mr. Rennert."

He was a small man, rather dapper, in a dark suit from whose buttonhole peeked a tiny white carnation. His face was oval and delicately featured, with well-cared-for, dark-olive skin. His teeth gleamed in white even rows beneath a diminutive waxed mustache.

"And Mr. Roark, of the United States Embassy," Fogarty continued.

The man turned a little sharply to Roark, and it was a moment before he extended his hand.

His quick black eyes roved over the other's face. "Ah yes, Mr. Roark. I think that I have met Mr. Roark, no?"

"Yes," the latter said evenly, "I met you here about six weeks ago."

"Certainly. You are interested in archaeology, Mr. Roark?"

"Not a great deal. Mr. Rennert here is."

Echave turned slowly to Rennert as if he were on a pivot, but Fogarty had forestalled him.

"And this is my assistant, Mr. Weikel, gentlemen."

Weikel rubbed his palm on his corduroy trousers before he extended it. Rennert could see now that his tanned face was blotched with pimples and that there was a reddish glint to his bristlelike hair.

He said not a word as he shook hands with them, but his small, deep-set, china-blue eyes met theirs in a blank, hostile stare.

Rennert broke the silence by turning to Echave. "I'm glad of this opportunity to talk to you. I'm down here to check up on the shipments which Dr. Fogarty has been sending to the Teague Museum. There was an accident to the last one, and some of the cases were broken."

He paused to observe the effect of his words.

Echave had turned so that his back was to the door, but even in the gloom Rennert had detected the sudden narrowing of his lids.

"I understand that you examine all specimens sent to the United States," he went on, "and sign the permit for the Department of Archaeology. Is that correct?"

"That is correct," without inflection.

"You examined personally the last shipment and the previous one, which went to the border about two months ago? I believe you said two months ago, Doctor?" Rennert turned unexpectedly to Fogarty.

The latter, caught off guard, wasn't able to clear away the frown which corrugated his forehead.

"Yes, yes," he nodded, "about two months ago."

"I examined those two shipments," the Mexican said imperturbably.

"You knew about the forgeries of pottery which were discovered?"

"Dr. Fogarty told me of them, yes."

"How do you account for them?"

An eloquent shrug. "I do not account for them. A band of thieves, without doubt, who substitute these forgeries at the railway station or on the train."

"Has your department been notified of other instances of the kind?"

"There are always such cases here in Mexico." He raised a hand to finger the white, perfect flower in his lapel, glanced down at it for a second, then raised his eyes to Rennert's in the same level stare. "Was there a forgery in the last shipment, Señor Rennert?"

"It might be called a forgery."

"What?" Fogarty thrust himself forward. "You didn't tell me about that."

Rennert smiled. "You were in such a hurry, Doctor. One of the skeletons was not that of a prehistoric man."

Fogarty blinked. "Are you sure of that?"

"Positive."

Very deliberately and slowly Dr. Fogarty loosed a stream of profanity which, Rennert thought, came near to being a masterpiece of extemporaneous composition. He fell silent abruptly and sank back onto a workbench. His lips were set tightly, and his eyes roamed the dark corners of the room.

Rennert took occasion to shift his position so that he could get a better view of some sacks piled at the bottom of what had evidently once been a chute leading from a hay mow. They contained lime.

Lime. . . .

He turned suddenly to Weikel, who stood motionlessly a little distance away, and surprised the young man's eyes fixed with an unpleasant glint on Echave.

"Can you be of any assistance to us, Weikel?"

The heavy head moved back and forth, and the blue eyes came slowly to Rennert's face.

"No," he said, as if it were an exhalation of his breath.

Fogarty swung himself off the table and said in an obvious endeavor to be conciliating:

"See here, Mr. Rennert. This matter is more serious than I thought. We can't go into all the ins and outs of it here. You say you're staying with the Faudrees? Well, suppose you let us finish up our work here. I'll see you tonight or in the morning, and we'll talk it over. It's getting dark in here, and we won't be able to work much longer. Satisfactory?"

"Very well, Doctor. My room is across the hall from yours. Good evening, gentlemen." He let his eyes rest for a moment on Echave's face, then on Weikel's, and turned away.

He and Roark paused at the north end of the coach house. The young man was eying him curiously.

"I'd like to know what you saw in that figurine to interest you so," he said.

"Didn't it remind you of anything?"

"I can't say that it did."

"The head? The buttocks?"

"Oh, my God!" Roark swore softly. "Sure! The drawings on those letters."

"Exactly. The tormentor and the tormented in one piece of clay."

Unnecessarily, Roark passed his hand again over his smooth hair. "We don't have far to look for the artist, then, do we?"

"Not very far." Rennert's voice was grim. "Shall we move on?"

Ahead of them and a few feet to the left was the bougainvillaea-draped wall which marked the eastern boundary of the Faudree property. At its base the rains had cut a deep gully, exposing somewhat lighter soil.

Rennert walked over to this, considered, then jumped down into it. He spent several minutes in an examination of the bottom and sides, stooping, prodding stones with the toe of his shoe. He climbed out and stood dusting his hands.

"Roark," he said with a faint smile, "are you as incurably romantic as I am? Always hoping that one of these buried treasures *will* materialize?"

The other laughed. "You can't live in Mexico long and not get the fever. I once invested in a project to hunt for Montezuma's gold. But you don't mean to say you actually believe Monica's story?"

Rennert shook his head sadly. "I'd like to. I don't doubt that Echave found a coin here. But the Mexicans are right. One swallow doesn't make a summer—and one coin doesn't make a treasure." He glanced at the stairs set against the wall of the building. "I think that a look at Voice's belongings is next on our list, isn't it?"

They climbed to a small rickety landing at the second-floor level. Rennert took out the key and opened the door.

They entered a square room with bare walls and flooring. There was a window on the north, almost hidden by boxes and bulging sacks, trunks and broken furniture, stacks of ancient newspapers. It was the customary litter which accumulates from years of housekeeping, but there was an orderliness about the arrangement of the objects unusual in a place where things are thrust haphazardly. Rennert remembered the former attic transformed by Cornell into living quarters. Its refuse must have found a haven here.

In a cleared space before the south window stood a table and chair. In a corner were a wardrobe trunk, a battered suitcase, a brief cage and a portable typewriter.

The windowpane was dusty and festooned with cobwebs, so that a dreary half-light filtered through.

Directly opposite was another door. Rennert walked over and tested the knob.

It opened, and he peered into an empty loft, which had probably been the storage place of hay in the days when a family carriage rested below.

He recalled the ladder set in the wall of the former stables beneath. With a gesture to Roark to remain where he was, he ventured out upon the boards and tiptoed to the trap door above the chute. He knelt down there, his nostrils pricked by the dust, and listened to the murmur of voices which came up.

He inserted a finger in the handle of the door and very carefully raised it a fraction of an inch. It didn't loosen as much dust as he had expected.

Lying almost prone on the floor he held his ear to the crack.

He could hear Fogarty's voice, rather high and nervous: "About through, Karl?"

There was some response from Weikel and a brief period of silence.

Then Fogarty laughed and said:

"Let the rest go until morning, Karl. It's too dark in here to work." After a moment he added, "Señor Echave and I will finish up."

Rennert heard Weikel's boots thump over the bricks. Then, just as they died away, came Fogarty's fierce:

"Listen here, Echave, we've got to be careful. Careful as hell. Somebody has got suspicious. This fellow Rennert's not interested just in those forgeries. He's got something else up his sleeve."

The Mexican's *Yes* came slowly and deliberately. "He has, as you say, something up his sleeve. There have been inquiries—very discreet inquiries—from the United States Embassy about your shipments."

"There have? Good God! When?"

"Within the last few days."

Another long silence.

"Echave," Fogarty asked in a quiet voice, dangerously soft, "are you being perfectly square with me?"

"Square?"

"Yes. Honest."

The Mexican's laugh had a taunt in it. "And if I were not, my dear Doctor, what would you do?"

"I don't know," Fogarty said slowly, "just what I would do."

"There would be nothing to do. You are in my country, remember." Another laugh. "But let us not quarrel. I am—what is it?—square with you."

"I'll take your word for it—for the present. See here, we can't talk now, with Rennert snooping about. Meet me here tonight. Nine o'clock, say. We'll talk over what we're going to do."

"It is a long streetcar trip from the city, Doctor. I might prefer that you meet me there."

"With the negrita in the next room sleeping alone? Or have you tired of her?"

Echave's laugh was more pleasant. "Very well. I shall meet you here. At nine?"

"Yes. The door will be unlocked."

Rennert got up and walked back to the other room.

14
SHOT

ROARK WAS STANDING, hands thrust into his pockets, and regarding him with a fixed one-sided smile.

"We'll have to requisition a new suit for you at this rate."

Rennert brushed himself off and told of the conversation which he had overheard.

Roark's eyebrows went up. "So! I thought Fogarty didn't like the idea of our escorting him in. He knew Echave was there and didn't want us to see him."

Rennert nodded.

"If I had access to a telephone," he said, "I'd be tempted to throw diplomacy overboard and ask the police to help us."

"Why?"

"I'd like to have Echave followed. My bet is that he'll be active in the next few hours."

"Think I could do it?"

"No aspersions on your skill, but he knows you. What about that chauffeur of yours?"

"He always keeps detective magazines in the pocket of the car. He ought to have learned something."

"Suppose we let him try. There'll be no great harm done if he loses him. Echave evidently came out in a streetcar. If the man hurries he can catch the same car back to Mexico City."

"Good. I'll go tell him." Roark hastily consulted his watch. "I'll drive up to the plaza with him and bring the car back. I don't have to be in Mexico City for an hour or so yet. While I'm at it I can get your bag at the San Angel Inn. I'm not helping any by standing here."

Left alone, Rennert looked about him.

From a corner he dragged an old feather mattress, propped it against a stack of yellowed newspapers and stepped back. He brought out the revolver which Cornell had given him, took aim and fired.

As soon as he felt the ringing cease in his ears he knelt in the dust and sought the bullet. He found it embedded in the newspapers. He sealed it in a small envelope and slipped it into his left-hand vest pocket.

After surveying Voice's possessions once more he began with the suitcase. It was unlocked, and he soon had its contents spread upon the table. He sorted through odds and ends of clothing but found nothing of interest.

Next he examined the typewriter, a much-used machine of a popular make. On the back of a discarded envelope he typed out the alphabet and the numerals for comparison with the letter which had arrived after Voice's death.

As he put the typewriter back into its case he was thinking of that letter—and of Monica Faudree. Damn it, why had the woman been so secretive? He was inclined to doubt her assertion that she would have to search—

"Oh, it's you, Mr. Rennert!"

He turned to face Cornell Faudree.

There had been a note of relief in her voice. Relief which showed itself as well in the increasing ease of her smile and the softening of her eyes.

She came into the room and closed the door.

Rennert explained his mission there and the shot.

"It's perfectly all right," she assured him. "I heard it and thought I'd better investigate."

"I hope I haven't disturbed everyone."

"Oh no, I was probably the only one. The house is of stone, you know, so sounds don't enter very well. I happened to have a window open."

"I understand that it's no novelty to hear firing from the direction of the Pedregal."

"No, there's always someone hunting or else just shooting to hear the noise." She hesitated. "Where's Delaney?"

"He went up to the plaza. He'll be back shortly."

"Well, I'll leave you, Mr. Rennert. You're busy."

"I'd be glad to have you stay. What I was doing can wait. Won't you sit down?"

She sank into the chair and eyed the dust on the table and the floor. "This place needs cleaning, doesn't it? I don't think it has been touched since Mr. Voice used to come here."

"He made use of this room?"

"He'd come out here and read those old newspapers. A lot of them date back to the Civil War."

Rennert leaned against a corner of the table. It was the first time he had seen the girl's face with a measure of repose on it. It was more mature than he had thought at his first meeting with her, with confidence in the set of the chin and in the introspective eyes. The hauteur of the high-bridged nose was more apparent.

"Did Professor Voice have a key to this room?" he asked.

"Yes."

"I wonder if it's the same one your sister Lucy gave me?"

"No, that's another, I'm sure. I remember Monica saying it was strange he had gone off and taken that key and the house key with him."

"I don't suppose the house locks have been changed since then?"

She shook her head and stared for a moment at the floor. "No, they haven't. I see what you mean. The person who murdered him had and may still have his keys."

"Yes."

"I'll have the locks changed, though it's late now to be doing that."

Rennert was thinking not only of access to the house, but to the laboratory downstairs. With a key to this room, a person could go readily through the loft to the trap door, from which a ladder descended to the picks and shovels and lime. . . .

She raised her eyes and looked at him steadily. "Mr. Rennert, did John tell you of our suspicions about those threat letters?"

"Yes, I'm glad you persuaded him to do so."

"It was foolish not to. John's so scrupulous that he'd rather get into trouble himself than be disloyal to somebody he thought was a friend." There was a note of anger in her voice. "And Karl Weikel's no friend of his. I've told John that again and again, but he always wants to believe the best of everybody."

"Weikel seems a rather surly fellow."

"He is. And vindictive. John told you, too, about the forgeries in that other shipment he was in charge of?"

"Yes."

"Do you want my opinion?"

"Very much."

"I think Karl put those forgeries in to get John in trouble. It must have been done by someone here at the excavations. Karl's jealous of John, because John's a more conscientious worker. Dr. Fogarty knows that and gives him more responsibility. That's why he let him take the shipments to the border instead of Karl."

"Is it your idea that Weikel substituted another skeleton for the same reason?"

She frowned and held her lips pressed together for a moment.

"If that skeleton hadn't been Professor Voice's," she said with slow deliberation, "if it had been merely an old, unidentified one, I would say *Yes*. But as it is I don't know what to think. I'm being perfectly frank with you, Mr. Rennert, not holding anything back on account of scruples, like John. I wouldn't like to think of Karl as a murderer. He disliked Mr. Voice, and I'm sure he sent him those letters. But that doesn't necessarily mean that he killed him, does it?"

"No." Rennert eased his position on the table. "Miss Faudree, you're the first person I've talked with who has suggested that the letters and the murder of Voice might be the work of different persons."

"Am I? It's natural enough to link one with the other. And Karl had a double motive for the murder: dislike of Voice and the desire to harm John. But murder's such a terrible thing, Mr. Rennert!"

"I realize that. One doesn't like to associate it with young men in their twenties. I was talking with Roark about that this afternoon. I wondered whether I was indulging in middle-aged sentiment about youth's innocence."

"You had been in John's company, Mr. Rennert. That's conducive to such sentiment." There it was again—that tender but dispassionate note.

"Yes," he said, "I suppose it's really young fellows like him I always think of, not the other kind. How old is he, by the way?"

She said flatly, "I don't know."

A challenge, he analyzed it. If so, subtlety wasn't going to be of much avail in leading up to the information he wanted.

"That's an unusual thing to say about a person I've known as long as John, isn't it?" she said. "That I don't know his age."

"It's unexpected, I admit. Exactness in counting the years is so important at that stage of the game."

"I'm sure he's well under thirty."

"I have been interested in his speech. He's not from the Southwest, is he?"

He had been right. She turned and looked straight into his eyes. "I don't know where he's from. Are you satisfied?"

She forestalled his apology. "I can see that Lucy has been talking to you, Mr. Rennert, about John."

"There was something more." Quietly he repeated the conversation between Biggerstaff and Weikel in the hall.

As he spoke she rose and stood with the tips of her fingers pressed against the surface of the table. He saw the tightening of her lips in profile against the dim rectangle of light.

When he had concluded she turned to him. Her back was to the window, so that her eyes were in shadow, but he felt the intensity of their gaze.

She spaced her words: "Mr. Rennert, I don't know what Karl meant. I don't care. I have known John since last October. He has talked to me a great deal about his life at Southwestern University. I know that he enjoyed it there, that he made friends. He has never said a word to me about his life before that. Only once did I ever ask him about it. He told me nothing. He said it made no difference. I'll always be satisfied with that. If you knew him as well as I do, you would be satisfied also."

Her sudden burst of laughter was incongruously loud in that still, dim-lit room.

"Oh, it's silly to be so melodramatic about this, Mr. Rennert! Acting as if John had a deep, dark past. Let's stop it."

"Very well," he said. "No more melodrama."

She glanced at the window. "It's getting dark. I must be going."

"Do you want to take your revolver with you?"

She looked down at the gun which he held on his palm. "Why yes, if you're through with it."

"I am."

"I want you to have that bullet compared with the other as soon as possible, Mr. Rennert. I realize that I can't expect you to be certain until you have done that."

"I shall do so at the first opportunity.

He walked with her to the door.

She paused on the landing and scanned the horizon, where ink-black clouds were hurling spears of rain upon the mountains. The warmth had gone from the air.

"You say Delaney's coming back soon?" she asked.

"Yes, he should be here now."

"Tell him I'd like to see him before he goes, will you? It's been a long time since we had a talk. I'll be in my apartment, if he'd like to come up."

"I'll tell him."

Her gaze was on the house now. Its southern side loomed as dark as the face of the lava from which it had been quarried.

"Why, there aren't any lights on!" she exclaimed. "Not even in the kitchen. Didn't I understand Monica to say that you were staying to dinner?"

"Yes. I understand that something is wrong with the electricity."

"Oh!" She turned to him quickly. "Is that what Lucy said?"

"Yes."

She sighed, and her face looked suddenly wan and tired.

"Good luck, Mr. Rennert," was all she said.

Rennert watched her go down the stairs and start toward the house.

He went back to his work then, but his thoughts weren't on it. Her expression of confidence in Biggerstaff had been a valiant effort, but it hadn't been convincing. She had spoken more to reassure herself than him.

He eyed the brief case, but decided to let it wait until daylight.

He pulled the trunk closer to the window and swung open its doors.

On the left side were hangers, with two suits of a conservative cut shiny from wear. In their pockets he found a pencil stub, a soiled handkerchief, and a folded envelope, addressed to Professor Garnett Voice at San Angel. It had been postmarked at Southwestern University on April 21. It was empty, but on its back three columns of numbers had been written in a careful, precise hand.

Rennert struck a match and studied them.

The first column began with A3,400 and contained the consecutive numerals to A3,425. The second commenced with G735 and ran to G745. The last series was from P22,005 to P22,015.

He sank into the chair and stared for a long time at these figures, put down in all probability by the murdered man within the few days preceding his death.

He gave it up and went back to the trunk.

There were four drawers on the right side. The first three contained a few collars, handkerchiefs and socks, books and toilet articles.

The fourth was locked.

Rennert produced a small leather case and with the aid of an innocent-looking steel instrument soon had the drawer open.

It was shallow and contained papers. . . .

He turned around as Roark came in.

"Well," the latter said, "everything worked out fine. There was a streetcar waiting at the plaza. I pointed Echave out to the chauffeur, restrained him from putting on false whiskers and put him on. Your bag's out in the car. I didn't have a key, so couldn't take it to your room."

Roark pushed his hat back from his forehead and stared at the objects which Rennert was replacing. "What the . . . ?"

There were several lavishly illustrated magazines and a pack of post cards. The cards, their photography and subject matter were products of Paris. They were well thumbed.

"The professor wasn't absorbed in his work all the time, was he?" Roark laughed. "They look like good art work."

Rennert snapped the drawer shut.

"Extremely good," he said as he got a little wearily to his feet. "And I speak as a connoisseur."

Roark showed his surprise.

"A man in the customs service," Rennert explained, "sees so much of that in the luggage of college professors—and others."

15
OWL

ROARK TOSSED his hat on the bed.

"This telegram," he said, "was waiting for you at the inn."

Rennert lit the thin wax candle which had been placed on his secretary during his absence and by its weak light read the message through twice, with a deepening frown.

"It's from my friend at Southwestern University," he said after a moment. "The same man who sent me the other. 'Biggerstaff query started something,' he says. *'Registrar finds on further examination name on transcript of precious credits from Chicago University changed from Biggers to Biggerstaff. Stop. Making inquiry Chicago."*

Roark's eyes were speculative. "That same mystery about Biggerstaff's name keeps cropping up, doesn't it?"

Rennert nodded as he slipped the paper back into its envelope. He stared at the brim of Roark's hat on the white coverlet and considered a new puzzle which had presented itself. A detail which in other circumstances would not have been accorded a second thought was invested now with the importance of the unexplained.

Roark, too, evidenced troubled thought. The candlelight aged his face, etching dark lines about the eyes and hollowing the closely shaven flesh on the cheeks and under the slightly sagging lower lip. He seemed to feel the necessity of talking.

"It'd be ironic if Cornell had made a mistake now. Fallen in love with some fellow who's not what she thinks. I only saw Biggerstaff once before today, but I thought he'd make the right kind of husband for her. More brawn than brain, but clean and honest, without any vices. That's the kind of man she's meant for."

"She asked me to deliver a message to you."

Roark's eyes went quickly to his face. "To me?"

"Yes. She came out to the coach house before you returned. She said she would like to see you, that she would be in her apartment if you wanted to come up."

Roark looked away. His lips were compressed into a thin, hard line.

"Tell Cornell she's better off not seeing me any more," he said, staring at the wall. "She has got away from smoky rooms now. She'd better stay away, where the air's clean." He broke off and heaved one shoulder in a shrug. "I've got to be going. I told the chauffeur to make his report on Echave to you."

Rennert had bent over the bed and was unfastening the clasps of his gladstone. He felt the need of a normally active person for a task to occupy his hands while his mind was busy.

"I wonder," he said, "if you could verify something for me? I gathered from Dr. Fogarty's insinuation that Echave is a frequent nocturnal visitor to the room of Marta, the mulatto maid."

"So our puritanical professor said."

"Voice?"

"Yes. He told me about it the night I stayed here. He was in a white heat of indignation that almost made him forget the letters. He had gone to Lucy Faudree and asked her if she knew that Marta was receiving a man in her room. Said that he had seen him go in several nights. It seems Lucy told him politely but firmly to mind his own business." Roark laughed. "She even asked him how he came to be watching the woman's room."

Rennert had a pair of shoes in his hands and was giving unnecessary scrutiny to their black, polished toes.

"Typical of the puritan," he said dryly.

"It was my first contact with one for a long time. Voice sat in that chair for hours talking about other men's lechery. I felt like asking him why he wasn't a missionary. Lucy would have turned him out of the house if she'd heard his hints about Marta's place with the family."

"Her mulatto blood, I suppose."

"Yes. He'd made a study of miscegenation in the South. Had statistics about the number of mulattoes in each generation. He said all the talk about Negro mammies identifying themselves with their masters' families was perfectly true. But it wasn't for sentimental reasons. The slave quarters in the Old South were too near the back doors of the mansions. But you aren't interested in Marta's amorous experiences, are you?"

"Not as such. I'm interested in that coach house." Rennert fished into the depths of the gladstone. "There's one thing more I'd like to ask you about before you go."

"What's that?"

"The owls."

"The owls?" Roark seemed startled. He laughed again, this time with an attempt at derision which did not succeed. "You aren't taking that talk seriously, are you?"

Rennert had extracted a blue serge suit. He carried it to the wardrobe, put it on a hanger and came back. "I'm taking it every bit as seriously as you."

Roark smoked in silence for a moment. "You think I did?"

"I know you did. If you read my face when I was looking at the drawings on those letters, I have reciprocated whenever the *tecolotes* have been mentioned. I want you to tell me everything you can about them."

Roark watched Rennert shake out the folds of a dark-gray topcoat. "Voice told me about them the morning he came to the embassy. He said that the Pedregal was suddenly filled with them at night. He thought that it might be a band of desperadoes giving signals. But when I questioned him, he admitted that he had actually seen the *tecolotes*. He said that they flew against his window at night. He was very much frightened."

"Had he heard of the Mexican belief about them at that time?"

"Yes. He quoted the saying, 'When the *tecolote* cries, the Christian dies.' After I stayed here one night I couldn't blame him much. Now, I'm far from being imaginative, but it was exactly as he'd said. It sounded as if every *tecolote* in Mexico had come to the edge of the Pedregal. There was one of them in particular, in that cedar tree at the back of the house, making the most ungodly screeching I ever heard. Then, I'll swear, the damned thing *did* fly right up against the windowpane. I'll admit I was almost as frightened as Voice. I'd brought my revolver with me and managed to shoot it as it was flying away. That drove off the others, and we weren't bothered any more that night."

"Did you see the bird after you shot it?"

"Yes, we looked at it the next morning before we buried it at the base of the cedar tree."

"Was it an ordinary *tecolote*?"

"Yes, as far as I could see."

"Did Voice say how long he had been bothered in this way?"

"About a week, I believe he said. I got your point downstairs about the coincidence of the letters and the incursion of the *tecolotes*."

"I don't believe," Rennert said, "that it was a coincidence."

Roark's laugh was a bit nervous. "You're not suggesting anything supernatural, are you?"

"No, I'm satisfied we'll find a rational explanation."

Roark tamped out his cigarette and lit another. His eyes followed Rennert's progress across the room with a handful of shirts, underwear and socks. "Are you going to try and find the explanation tonight?"

"Yes."

"Can I be of any help?"

"I think not." Rennert pushed shut the drawer of the wardrobe and faced him. "You've done your part in getting me acquainted with the scene and the people here. It's my job from now on. As you can see, I'm settled in this room until I finish it."

"I can come back tonight or in the morning if you want me to." Roark picked up his hat and stood twirling it upon a finger.

"It's not necessary to come back tonight. I'd like to see you tomorrow."

"All right. I'll come out in the morning." Rennert took a card from his pocket and wrote on it. "Here's my address and phone number, in case you want to get in touch with me."

"Thanks."

Roark extended a hand. "Good night, Mr. Rennert."

"Good night."

When he had gone Rennert walked to the window.

Far away, at the base of the mountains which had confined the flow of the lava centuries ago, a single light had twinkled into being, emphasizing by its remoteness the extent of the wasteland between these two human habitations. In the one, a dark-skinned family grouped about a hearthfire, speaking a tongue which their ancestors had spoken before the white man saw this continent, following thought processes unintelligible to the foreigner who waited in this room for a summons to a polite and civilized meal. And between them, dark and unpassable, the lava.

Better now than ever before Rennert could understand the quality of the fear with which the Pedregal is endued by those who dwell on its fringes. In other places, even in the deserts of the north or on the bleak mountain peaks, man might die, but Nature lived fecundly on. Here Nature herself was dead. Never, in any cycle of the planet, would a flower or a blade of grass grow on this dead sea of stone. Small wonder that Malinche, when she returns at night to the land which she loved and betrayed, should seek this spot to keen her sorrow. . . .

The window was narrow and high, with leaded panes. Rennert pushed up the lower sash and leaned out. The air was damp, already impregnated with the night chill of the Mexican uplands.

The sound of Roark's car was already dying, on the road that leads to the plaza of San Angel and the lights and clatter of Mexico City.

Directly below him was the window of Lucy Faudree's room, on either side the blank surface of the wall. The gutter at the edge of the roof was at least eight feet above his head. From the window frame above the upper sash a nail projected. Something dangled from it.

Rennert drew back into the room and pulled down both sashes. Taking a packet of matches from his pocket he rested his foot on the sill and, with the painful realization that such acrobatic feats were for younger, slimmer men, hoisted himself into a sitting posture half in, half out of the window.

He thrust his head out, struck a match and, holding it carefully cupped in his left hand, raised it. The nail was deeply imbedded in the wood. From it hung an inch or so of string, frayed at the end.

He perched there, uncomfortably, until the flame of the match approached his skin. Flicking the stub into the night he swung himself back into the room and closed the window.

When the tinkle of chimes echoed through the hall, he had his coat off and was engaged in strapping a leather holster under his left armpit. In the holster nestled a small but dependable revolver.

This constituted his dressing for dinner.

16
YAWN

"THE WEATHER," Lucy Faudree said, "always surprises foreigners in Mexico for the first time. They can't understand that summer and winter don't mean hot and cold with us, but wet and dry."

"It's partly the fault of the tourist companies," Rennert said. "Those in the North particularly. Their appeal is to people who want a change from cold and dampness. So they play up the balmy sunshine of Mexico, regardless of the geographical variations here."

Silence fell on the table. Rennert had felt it edging in on them since the beginning of the meal—that special silence, charged with tension, which comes between people who are constrained from voicing the only thoughts which they have in common. Never an accomplished conversationalist in circumstances such as this, this brief preliminary skirmish with the subject of the weather left him temporarily at a loss.

Lucy sat at the head of the table, her thin, straight shoulders dwarfed by the high-backed chair. She ate little, and her gaze kept going to the still flames of the two tall red candles as if fascinated by their steady diminution.

She looked up as if suddenly aware of her lapse. Her eyes seemed extraordinarily bright. "We must have some wine, Mr. Rennert. I very seldom drink it, but I think that under the circumstances . . ."

She left the sentence unfinished, but raised the tiny bell which rested on a lace doily by her right hand. Its tinkle sounded singularly

110

inadequate in that large room, with its dark wainscoted walls rising to a dimly perceived ceiling.

She looked over Rennert's shoulder and said to Marta, who had entered with a soft swish of skirts: "Some rioja, please, Marta."

"Rioja is all that is needed to make this Brunswick stew perfection, Miss Faudree," Rennert said.

It was the first time that evening that he had seen spontaneousness in her smile. "I'm so glad you like it. It's one of our traditional Southern dishes. Perhaps you have eaten it in the South?"

"Yes, although usually I have to depend upon a restaurant version."

"You are a bachelor, then, Mr. Rennert?"

"Yes."

For some reason the word sounded too rotund and decisive, effectually blocking further ingress upon this subject. He was trying to think of some way to continue when Marta came in again. She was carrying, with an almost sacerdotal air, an antique purple bottle. She began to pour the deep-red liquid into Lucy's glass.

The latter stopped her in a moment. "That's enough, Marta."

It was while his own glass was being filled that the hall door opened and Monica entered.

"Wine!" she exclaimed as she walked toward the table. "My, this *is* an occasion."

Her face was slightly flushed, from agitation or haste. She wore the same dress but had attached white lace collar and cuffs. Both were awry, and she was worrying with the right sleeve as Rennert held her chair for her.

"Oh, thank you," she said breathlessly. "I'm so sorry to be late, but I've had the most distressing time."

"You have?" he inquired politely.

"Yes. I sat with Mr. Biggerstaff while he slept. I looked out the window and watched the rain clouds gradually blot out the sun. I got to thinking how symbolic it was and composed a little poem. His young life was the sun. Ardent, you know, and full of promise. The clouds were the deep sleep that he was in, that covers a person just as if—well, just as if he were dead. But then, in the morning, the sun— Oh yes, thank you, Mr. Rennert, I *will* have some Brunswick stew. And just a bit more wine, Marta, please."

As the gold bracelet slipped down the warm, dark flesh of Marta's wrist toward the glass into which she was pouring the rioja, the candle flames flared suddenly, sagged and slowly righted themselves. The walls seemed to recede and advance with the shifting shadows. A draft of cold air touched Rennert's ankles. It came, he judged, from the rear door, through the kitchen and across the narrow intervening hall.

Lucy said dryly, "The dinner chimes rang, Monica, at the usual time."

"Oh yes, I know. Will you please set this down, Mr. Rennert? Thank you. Yes, I heard the chimes. I hadn't realized, you see, how late it had got. I hurried across to my room, then, to—well, to tidy up a bit. And it was so dark in there, with only a candle, that I couldn't find a handkerchief. It was the strangest thing. I always keep my handkerchiefs in a little box in the upper right-hand drawer of my dresser. With sachets between them. I keep my work-bag in the same drawer, so I knew that box had been there when I went to Mr. Biggerstaff's room about an hour before. But it wasn't there when I came back. It gave me the oddest feeling, just as if there were little brownies about playing their tricks. And where do you think I found it?"

She sipped wine and looked about the table expectantly.

No one said anything.

There was something definitely forced in her exuberance. Her fingers kept playing with the stem of the glass, as if she were unable to set it down.

"Well, I found it in the upper *left*-hand drawer. Just stuck in carelessly with—with some other things. And I'm sure that it was the upper right-hand drawer I put it in. I always do. And when I opened it I found all the sachet envelopes on top of the handker-chiefs and not in between, as I always lay them. And one of them was torn open. The powder had sifted down into everything. But the strangest thing was that I found some more of that same pow-der in a little pile on the carpet by the window. And I'm positive that I never had that box near the window. There wouldn't be any reason for my carrying it over there, would there, Mr. Rennert?"

Rennert was regarding her thoughtfully. He was sure that it was no effect of the lighting which made her eyes appear so heavy, their pupils almost torpid.

"No, Miss Faudree," he said. "Unless you wanted to take the box to a place where you could see better. You may have done that and forgotten about it."

"But, Mr. Rennert, I know I didn't. It wasn't dark when I went in Mr. Biggerstaff's room. And besides, I didn't touch the box then."

The back door slammed, and the candle flames shuddered again in the current of air which went through the room. Heavy booted feet clumped up the stairs to the second floor.

Lucy's voice came cool and a bit sharp from the other end of the table:

"You forget, Monica, that Mr. Rennert isn't interested in these little intimate details, such as which drawer you put your hand-kerchiefs in."

"But he is! I can tell by his face that he is."

Rennert said, "I am very much interested, Miss Faudree. How large are these sachet envelopes you keep the powder in?"

"Oh, they're just ordinary correspondence envelopes. I get the powder in big cans and then put it in envelopes. It goes so much farther that way."

"So that at dusk a person might mistake them for letters?"

"Why yes, I suppose so. But . . ." Monica laid down the fork with which she had been playing with a morsel of chicken and raised her napkin. But not quickly enough to cover a yawn.

Lucy's laugh was clear, bell-like almost. "You are a perfect bachelor, Mr. Rennert. You can pretend interest so convincingly in little feminine foibles. If you were a married man, now, it would be impossible. They would be such commonplaces to you."

Rennert had to make an effort to answer calmly. "Perhaps, Miss Faudree, I'm interested because, being a bachelor, I often mislay my own handkerchiefs. I have some hectic moments, I assure you, getting to the office in the morning."

The rain stopped further conversation for the moment. It came suddenly, without the accompaniment of thunder or lightning, drumming upon the ground and setting the windows to rattling with the violence of its impact.

"Oh, speaking of handkerchiefs, I remember an anecdote my father used to relate . . ."

Lucy talked on, resolutely, against the crescendo beat of the rain.

Rennert heard someone descend the rear stairs, heard the back door close and felt the draft again on his ankles.

His attention, however, was upon Monica. Twice she leaned back in her chair and let her eyes close for an instant. Their lids looked puffy, as if she were drugged by sleepiness. Each time she suppressed a yawn and began again on her food. At last she gave it up and sat, her shoulders slack, staring listlessly at the candles.

Finally Lucy glanced at her sister sharply and laid down her napkin. "Shall we go into the parlor now? Marta will bring our coffee to us there."

As Monica rose one of her hands caught the back of her chair, while the other brushed over her eyes.

Rennert fell into step beside her as they passed into the hall.

"There's a question I want to ask you about that gold coin which you saw, Miss Faudree." He tried to speak naturally. "You said that it had a date. Do you remember what it was?"

The only illumination was the candlelight which came from behind them and through the open door of the parlor opposite, but he could see the muscles at the corners of her mouth move as if she were about to draw in her cheeks. She said thickly:

"Oh yes, the date. I associated it with something. Let's see. What could it have been? Something in United States history."

"Was it, by any chance, the Declaration of Independence?"

Her steps were slowing. "Yes. That was it. 17 . . ."

"1776," he said for her.

She had stopped at the door of the parlor. "I wonder if you'd mind if I went upstairs and lay down for a while? I don't feel very well."

He said quickly, "Let me help you."

"No, no, don't bother, Mr. Rennert." Her reply was indistinct. "I'm just sleepy. I—I don't think I should have drunk that wine."

Alarmed, he watched the darkness of the landing envelop her.

17
CREAK

MONICA WONDERED what was wrong with herself.

It had come over her so suddenly, this leaden drowsiness which was weighing down her eyelids and setting up a humming far back in her head. The distances between the treads of the stairs seemed to have lengthened, too, so that it took increasing exertion to lift her feet from one of them to the next. She thought of her bed as a haven toward which she was moving with nightmare slowness.

She gained the upper hall and paused for breath. There was no light at all, but she knew her way from a lifetime of experience.

She opened her door, but kept her hand on the knob for several seconds, bothered by the darkness which confronted her. Despite the confusion of her mind, she was sure that she had left a candle burning on top of the dresser. It had been such a small extravagance, and Lucy would never know of it.

She groped across the room. Her fingers touched hot wax, and she withdrew them quickly. Odd that the sides of the candle should have stayed so hot if she had blown it out when she left. But no, she was sure she hadn't done that. It must have been a draft, although the window was closed. She found a packet of matches, lit one and applied it to the wick.

The yellow light struggled out over the room, projecting shadows crazily.

She looked about her, vaguely uneasy. But everything was as she had left it. The big four-poster bed on one side of the door, with its embroidered coverlet of which she was so proud. On the other side of the dresser a rocking chair, a low bookshelf and, by the south window, the wardrobe, like the one in Mr. Rennert's room. Its two long glass panels were closed, and she could see her reflection in it, slightly distorted.

A small clock ticked away, very faintly, on the dresser. She had to strain her eyes to see its face.

Only seven-forty.

It was nonsense to go to bed this early. She wanted to see Mr. Rennert again, to give him that letter which he was so anxious to get. He had been so nice and polite about it.

She went to the bookcase and took out a thick album bound in deep-purple plush with her initials stamped on the cover in gold.

She carried it to the dresser and laid it beside the candle. She opened it and found a certain page upon which a sheet of notepaper was pasted by one of its edges, so that it could be turned to either side.

Face downward was the typewritten letter which Mr. Rennert wanted.

> Dear Miss Faudree:
> An unexpected development makes it necessary
> for me to return to the United States at once. I am
> not sure at present how long

Without finishing it she carefully removed the sheet. It was of no more interest to her, now that she knew it hadn't been written by Mr. Voice. This knowledge rather spoiled, too, the pleasurable sensation which she had derived from reading the lines of poetry which she had written on the reverse side.

"Words at Parting," she had called the little poem. The beginning had come to her suddenly the morning she read the letter. As always, on such occasions, she had sat down immediately to put them on paper. It was so hard to regain that first exciting moment of inspiration if one let it pass. In fact she usually carried a little pencil and a slip of paper in her pocket for that very purpose, as she had read so many poets did. This time, however, it had been more appropriate to write on the back of the letter which had been the cause of those words slipping into her mind.

> *Words at meeting*
> *Are so fleeting . . .*

She brought out her pencil and began to erase them. Of course she could have explained to Mr. Rennert about how she came to write a poem on the back of the letter. She had observed that an almost dreamy look came into his eyes sometimes. Undoubtedly he would have a feeling for poetry, despite the rather imposing bulk of his masculinity. But it might be necessary for him to show the letter to someone else. Lucy perhaps. And Lucy was always ridiculing her poetry. . . .

Her eyelids were beginning to sag again. She laid down the pencil with numb fingers.

She decided to go to the bathroom, dash cold water on her face.

She got to the door and turned.

The rain was slapping against the windowpane and rattling in a loose gutter overhead. There had been a faint creaking, too. In the wardrobe, evidently. The wood expanding as it always did at the beginning of the rainy season.

She went out and crossed to the bath.

She stayed there for several minutes. When she came out she felt a little better: her head was clearer.

The door of John Biggerstaff's room was only a few feet from her right hand now. She considered for a moment, then tiptoed to it.

John had looked so young, lying there in his sleep. It was almost amusing to see the dark stubble on his cheeks and lips, showing that he had not shaved recently. It was difficult to think of John being Cornell's husband someday, holding her in his strong arms. . . .

Very softly she opened the door and went in, shading the candle with one hand. Unaccountably she felt a warm little glow of happiness.

The bedclothes were rumpled, the way John always disturbed them with those muscular legs of his. But John wasn't in the bed.

She took her hand from the candle flame to make sure that her eyes were not deceiving her. She looked about the room. She did not find the dressing gown which had been hung over the foot of the bed or the slippers which had lain on the floor when she had sat there before dinner.

Mr. Rennert must have been mistaken about that sedative when he said that John would sleep until morning. And where could he have gone? Not to the bathroom, because she had just come from there. . . .

She couldn't control her yawn. It gripped her jaws and sent a delicious feeling of relaxation through her.

After all, if one was sleepy, one was sleepy. It was silly to force oneself to wakefulness on account of a letter which could just as well wait until morning.

She crossed the hall to her own room, put down the candle and began the impossible task of undressing. She removed the collar and the cuffs and replaced them in a drawer.

As she turned, her eyes fell on the wardrobe. While she had been gone the doors had come entirely open, exposing the disarray of her dresses inside. She never left her garments pushed together on their hangers in that way.

But it was too much of an effort to straighten them now. It was too much of an effort to continue undressing, even.

She went as swiftly as she could to the bed. If she could only get her head down on the pillow and close her eyes for a moment nothing else mattered.

She slept at once.

18
SLEEP

RENNERT SAT in the pool of light cast by the candles and watched Lucy lean over a low table, inlaid with mosaic, which bore a spirit lamp and a coffee service. Her fingers looked as white and fragile as the china cups she was moving about. She was saying:

"Now, Mr. Rennert, we can resume our conversation of this afternoon. I always prefer not to discuss unpleasant matters at dinner. Don't you?"

"Certainly."

"After you left I went back over the days when Mr. Voice was receiving those letters. I tried to think of something that might help you. I remembered one incident which may or may not be of importance. Do you use cream and sugar, Mr. Rennert?"

"Neither, thank you."

"This happened on the night of May first. I don't know exactly what time, but it was late. I had been kept awake by the shots but had finally fallen asleep." She handed him a cup.

"The shots?" he prompted.

"Yes. May Day has got to be a time of fiesta here in Mexico. The radical element is so strong, you know." She shrugged deprecatingly. "And then, too, the religious celebrations are being discouraged, so May Day takes their place. There is always a great deal of *pulque* consumed, with consequent disturbances. Fireworks, gunfire and so forth."

Rennert nodded, wondering whether it was by accident or design that a bullet had pierced a man's head on a night when one more shot would have attracted no attention.

"On that night," Lucy went on, "a windowpane of Mr. Voice's room was broken. I was awakened by the shattering of glass. I was confused for a moment or two, the way one is. I got up, however, and went to the window. The light was on in the room above, and Mr. Voice was leaning out. I called him and asked if anything was wrong. He acted startled but said that he had accidentally broken the pane. I went back to bed. That was the last time I saw him. The letter came the next day."

"Was he dressed when you saw him at the window?"

"Yes. Evidently he had just returned."

"Returned?"

"My memory seems to be improving, doesn't it? Mr. Voice had gone to Mexico City that evening."

"At what time?"

"Soon after dinner. He came to my room and asked if I had a copy of that day's newspaper. I did. He looked up something in it, then said he was going in to Mexico City."

"You have no idea what it was he looked up?"

"No."

"How did he seem—excited, pleased, displeased?"

She thought for a moment. "I didn't observe him carefully, but I think he was excited. Yes, I'm sure he was. He kept glancing at his watch."

Rennert sipped coffee from a thin white cup which had a nick on the rim. The coffee was hot and strong, and bitter with chicory, but it didn't seem to combat the nervousness which kept impelling him to turn his head and listen for sounds from the hall or from upstairs. The rain splashed away against the windows, so that the hush in the house was by comparison undisturbed. He had to admit himself too distracted to concentrate properly on this new and, he felt, vital bit of information. He craved a cigarette but knew that it would be futile to look for an ash tray in this room.

"May I ask a few more questions, Miss Faudree?"

"Of course. Anything you wish."

"As you said this afternoon, there are always owls in the Pedregal. But it is true, isn't it, that they were particularly active while Voice was receiving those letters?"

She put down her cup and reached up to draw the cashmere shawl about her shoulders.

"It is, Mr. Rennert. I heard them myself. They would gather on the edge of the Pedregal nearest the house and in the cedar tree at the back. Several nights I heard them fly to his window. That is a simple statement of fact, unembroidered by imagination. I tried to dismiss it with a laugh, but I couldn't."

"Do you recall the approximate period of time over which you heard the *tecolotes?*"

"They must have begun about a week before May first."

"And did you hear them after that?"

"I heard them sometimes, far out on the lava, but they never came again so near the house."

"Did you have any explanation?"

Her fingers began to move down the fringe of the shawl, tugging methodically at the little knots in turn.

"I thought at first that a new kind had migrated here. But the night Mr. Roark stayed with us he shot one. I went out and looked at it the next morning before he buried it. It was the ordinary kind one sees about here. I decided then that some roosting place of theirs out on the Pedregal must have been broken up. They stopped bothering us, and I thought no more about them."

Rennert leaned forward. "Did Professor Voice know about the superstition that the *tecolote's* cries precede death?"

Her eyes moved restlessly about, pausing momentarily on the mantel ledge, on the two gilt-framed silhouettes on the wall beside it, on the steady flame of the nearer of the two candles. It was as if she were seeking something to hold her gaze. "Yes, it worried him more than he would admit, I think."

"Did he know about it before they started, or did someone tell him?"

Her fingers had reached the end of the shawl's black fringe. They remained for a moment fluttering over her lap, then sought the chair arms, to move along the gilt nailheads in the upholstery.

"I think," she said deliberately, "that someone told him. Yes, I'm sure of it. He asked Marta; said that someone had told him that the *tecolotes* always gave warning of death."

"And Marta assured him that they did?"

"Yes. Marta is very intelligent in most ways, but she has any number of foolish beliefs locked away in the back of her mind. Her grandmother was a Faudree slave who came down with the family. Her mother married and left us to live in Mexico City. She brought Marta back to us when she was in her teens, after she had absorbed a great deal of superstition." She paused. "Oh, while I think of it, Mr. Rennert. You asked to see the letters which Mr. Voice was studying. I have them here."

From a table she took a packet of yellowed envelopes bound by a rubber band.

"I'm not sure," she said as she gave it to him, "just what you will find. It has been some time since I looked at them. But I think they're mostly letters which my grandfather and his family received before and during the war. I had always supposed they concerned personal matters, of interest only to ourselves. But Mr. Voice assured me that there were some from prominent men, and that they threw a great deal of light on the war. The Faudrees had connections and friends throughout the South."

"Thank you. I shall return them as soon as possible. Now let me thank you for a most pleasant dinner." (It was impossible to sit still any longer, assuring himself that one glass of wine had been responsible for Monica's drowsiness.)

"You are gracious, Mr. Rennert. But I know that the thoughts of both of us have been elsewhere." She paused. "I don't want to annoy you with questions, but tell me this: Are you making progress?"

"A great deal, Miss Faudree."

She stared at the floor. "I have lived in this house all my life, Mr. Rennert. I know every inch of it as I know my own conscience. But tonight I feel as if I were a stranger in it. These walls, the furniture, my grandfather's picture, even—all seem different." Her voice became strained. "I lived through the Revolution. I remember the rumors of danger, the shots in my ears day and night, the sight of butchered men in the streets. I wasn't afraid then, as long as I was within these walls. I knew that I was safe. But now I feel as if something had got into this house. Something evil that has

changed the things I know. It started when you came this afternoon, Mr. Rennert. I don't blame you, but I am wondering if perhaps it would not be wise to stop any further investigation, to let
the dead past bury its dead."

She looked up and met his steady gaze. He was standing so that
the candlelight fell full on the long tanned line of his jaw and on
his firm, severe chin.

"Is that your wish, Miss Faudree?" he asked quietly.

She laughed nervously and passed a hand across her forehead.
"No, no." She shook her head. "Of course not. I was forgetting
myself. I wasn't reasonable. You must go ahead, of course."

"And you will trust me to act as I think best here in your house
tonight?"

"Yes."

"Thank you. Now—"

"You must be going, I know. Take one of those candles to light
your way upstairs."

He knew that her eyes were on his back as he went out.

He paused in the upper hall and surveyed the tight-shut doors
which faced him. The beat of the rain was muffled here, as if the
dark, distempered walls enclosed a private stillness of their own.

He went to the door of Monica's room and knocked lightly.

There was no response.

He knocked again, waited, and turned the knob. He stood on
the threshold and looked about him.

A half-burned candle stood on the dresser, a yellow cascade of
wax dripping down one side. Monica Faudree lay on the bed fully
dressed. She looked old and not a little ludicrous, with her breath
coming stertorously through her partially opened mouth and the
lenses of her spectacles giving back an opaque reflection of the
light.

He called to her sharply, then went to the bed and caught her
by the shoulder. He shook her several times. She moaned slightly,
and her breathing became irregular. But she did not waken.

CORNELL HAD BEEN CRYING, Rennert saw as soon as the girl opened her door to his knock.

She did not avert her eyes from the candle quickly enough to hide the glistening brightness of their pupils or the redness of their lids.

"I'm a bit worried about your aunt Monica," he said. "Can you come with me to her room?"

"Monica?" She took away the handkerchief with which she had been touching her mouth and nose. "What's the matter?" Concern for herself was gone now, and she looked straight at him.

"She became sleepy at dinner and went to her room to lie down. I thought it best to knock at her door a few moments ago and assure myself that she was all right. I can't waken her."

"Why, of course, Mr. Rennert." Cornell stepped into the hall and closed the door.

He followed her into the nearby room, watched her repeat his actions of calling and shaking Monica.

The cords of her throat were tight as she turned to him and tried to laugh. "This is strange. She seems all right, except that she's sleeping so soundly. It's as if—she were drugged, or something."

"Exactly. Will you undress her, get her to bed and stay with her for a time? Later we can attempt to rouse her, if we think it best."

"Why surely." He saw the slow widening of her eyes and the accentuation of their brightness. Her face was white. "You think that someone did this to her—on purpose?"

125

"It appears so, Miss Faudree. When was the last time you saw her?"

"When you and John and Mr. Roark were in my apartment. She stayed a few minutes after you left."

"I have to ask this question. Did she eat or drink anything while there?"

She shook her head. "No, nothing at all. I'm sure of that."

"Very well. One more thing. Did you know that she had saved the letter which came to Lucy about the first of May with the signature of Professor Voice?"

"No."

"Do you know where she might keep such a letter?"

Her gaze wandered about the room. "No. In a drawer of her dresser, perhaps. Or in the wardrobe."

Rennert stepped over to the dresser and looked at the album which lay there. The page which met his eyes was blank, but there was a thin line of dried paste down the left side.

Swiftly he went through the book, glancing at the lines written with pen or pencil, at the saint's day and Christmas cards pasted there. He found no typewritten missive.

He turned to Cornell. "Does anyone in the house own a typewriter?"

"Dr. Fogarty has one."

"No one else?"

"No. I know that because both boys, John and Karl, use it. I've even borrowed it myself."

Rennert left the album and moved toward the door, whose key was on the inside.

"Is your aunt in the habit of locking her door?" he asked.

"Usually at night, I think. But not in the daytime. There's no need. Things like this—just don't happen to us, Mr. Rennert."

"And I trust they won't again. I'll leave you now. It might be well to keep this door locked until I return."

"All right." Her voice was steadier now. "You think there's danger, don't you?"

"Not for her—" he stared at the bed—"now. But I don't want to take any more chances."

He waited in the hall until he heard the key turn in the lock, then crossed to Weikel's room.

The young man was wearing the same corduroy trousers and faded blue shirt, but had removed his boots and put on bedroom slippers.

He stood unbudging in the doorway and regarded his visitor with a level stare. The candlelight gave a bilious hue to his skin and made the pimples on his cheeks stand out in bold relief.

"Good evening," Rennert said. "I want to talk to you, Weikel."

The other stood a moment longer, saying nothing, then stepped aside.

"Come in," he said grudgingly.

Rennert entered, set his candle on the table and moved the straight chair about so that he could face Weikel.

"Sit down." He gestured toward the rocker. When Weikel had lowered his cumbrous body into the chair, Rennert went on:

"I intended to call on you sooner but thought I'd give you time to eat your dinner. Where do you fellows take your meals, by the way?"

There was something in Weikel's unusually small eyes which Rennert couldn't quite analyze. It wasn't altogether antagonism, despite the forbidding aspect of the heavy, drawn brows and the lack of a smile on the lips. An uncertainty and wariness, rather.

"Up on the plaza," he answered.

"At a restaurant?"

"Yes. El Chico. *I* eat there," he amended.

"Dr. Fogarty and Mr. Biggerstaff don't?"

"No. It's not good enough for them. They eat at El Eliseo. That's more expensive."

All this had come readily enough. There had even been a trace of eagerness in the replies.

"I see. At what time did you go to dinner tonight?"

"About six-thirty."

Rennert glanced at the boots which stood at the foot of the bed. "You got back before the rain started, I judge."

"Just did."

Rennert remembered the second flare of the candles in the draft from the rear door and the heavy footsteps on the stairs as they had sat at the dinner table. Something in the way of corroboration. . . .

"Weikel," he said, "Dr. Fogarty has told you that I am with the United States Customs Service. You heard my questions out in the coach house. Have you thought of anything in the meantime which might help me?"

Weikel's eyes were guarded now.

"No," he said at once. "I'm only Dr. Fogarty's assistant. I don't know anything."

"Diego Echave is perfectly trustworthy, isn't he?"

Weikel shrugged and said tonelessly:

"I suppose so. I don't know. You'll have to ask Dr. Fogarty."

Rennert asked in the same manner, "Did you know Professor Garnett Voice?"

Save for a quickened rise and fall of his nostrils that bespoke accelerated breathing, Weikel's facial expression did not change.

Rennert waited and, when no reply seemed forthcoming, repeated his question.

"Yes, I knew him." It was said with a slight tightening of the lips, so that it sounded almost like a sneer.

"You knew him at Southwestern University, didn't you?"

"Yes."

"When was the last time you saw him?"

"I don't remember. A long time ago. A month or six weeks."

"Did you know about the threatening letters he received?"

Weikel raised an arm and ran his sleeve over his forehead as if to remove invisible perspiration. "Yes, I knew about them."

"Do you know who sent them?"

"No."

"Are you sure?" Rennert was regarding him steadily.

Weikel stared straight in front of him and repeated the monosyllable doggedly.

"I've learned about the trouble you had with Voice at Southwestern University," Rennert pursued quietly. "The Phi Beta Kappa election."

Weikel glanced up quickly, then leaned forward, his hands propped on his knees, to gaze at the floor.

"So that's why you're here, is it?" he said through half-shut white teeth. "Voice has gone to the police. Well, you can tell him to be damned. He hasn't got any proof I sent those letters. He can't pin anything on me." He laughed, a little wildly and with a rasping sound.

"Voice has not gone to the police."

Weikel looked up. "He hasn't?"

"Voice was murdered near this house the night of May first. After he had received two letters threatening him with death if he didn't pay a sum of money. After he had been frightened by owls flying to his windows at night. His body was buried and covered with lime. It was dug up recently, put into a plaster cast and sent off to the United States with the skeletons which John Biggerstaff took up. That's why I'm here."

Weikel had lifted himself half out of his chair. His breath came and went in quick, tearing gasps. He seemed incapable of speech. There was no mistaking the emotion in his eyes now. It was stark, undisguised fear.

"You must realize the seriousness of your predicament, Weikel. Do you have any statement to make?"

The other sank back into the chair and shook his head.

Rennert waited for several seconds, until the clangor of the knocker on the front door reverberated through the house.

He rose then. "Pardon me a moment. I'm going to ask you that same question when I come back." He caught up his candle and went down the stairs.

At the front door he found the chauffeur from the embassy. The young Mexican was a solid and cheerful figure, smiling in disregard of the rivulets of water which trickled from his hatbrim.

"Good night," he said in slow, painstaking English as he stepped inside. "You are Mr. Rennert, no?"

"Yes. You have a report on Echave?" Rennert repressed the shiver which came on contact with the raw night air.

"Yes, mister. I go to the plaza with Mr. Roark in the automobile. We stop near the tranvías—the streetcars. Mr. Roark talks to Echave so that I know who he is. Then I wait. Echave enters in the tranvía. I enter in the—"

"Hablemos español," Rennert interrupted kindly.

The other seemed disappointed but went on more swiftly in his own language. Upon his arrival in Mexico City Echave had gone at once to the offices of the Department of Archaeology. He had remained there about twenty minutes. Then he had taken a taxi to an address far out on the Paseo de la Reforma, near Chapultepec. This was an old family residence, the chauffeur had ascertained, where lived one Moises Sart. After about half an hour Echave had come out and returned in the taxi to the Zócalo, where he boarded the San Angel car.

Rennert's questions brought out the fact that Roark's instructions to the man had been that he need not follow his quarry farther. Consequently the chauffeur had dined and returned to San Angel in no great haste to make his report. This meant that Echave had preceded him by forty-five minutes or more.

Rennert frowned. This had not been according to his plan. He had wanted Echave's movements accounted for not only in Mexico City but in San Angel as well. His face was thoughtful as he thanked the man, tipped him and dismissed him.

He looked at his watch. Eight twenty-five. Where, he wondered as he went up the stairs, was Echave now?

He found Weikel sitting in the same abject posture. The fellow raised dull eyes as Rennert entered.

The latter did not resume his seat but stood with folded arms. "I'm repeating that question, Weikel. Do you have a statement to make?"

There was no reply. Only a desperate tightening of the large splayed fingers on the chair arms.

"I have those letters which were sent to Voice." Rennert's tone was incisive. "They were printed, you remember. There on the table are some pieces of pottery, with labels on which numbers and letters are printed. I think that an expert might be able to determine whether or not they correspond. I have taken some of them for comparison."

Up the stair well came the sound of the closing of the rear door.

"I'm going to leave you alone for a few minutes, Weikel. Understand this: the matter has not been turned over to the police as yet. Anything you say to me will be treated confidentially if I think best. I should advise you to do some thinking while I'm gone. Some damned hard thinking."

Rennert went out and closed the door.

He was in time to meet Dr. Fogarty at the head of the stairs. The archaeologist held a flashlight and a hat in one hand, and was unbuttoning his raincoat with the other, shaking himself meanwhile like a large Newfoundland dog. He looked ill-tempered as he grunted an unintelligible greeting.

"I've been waiting for you, Doctor," Rennert said.

20
PICK

"WAITING FOR ME?" Fogarty seemed to address the raincoat, which he had stripped off and was holding at arm's length.

He bent over and slapped at his damp trouser legs. "Oh yes, about those specimens."

He straightened up. "Come in my room. Rennert, I believe you said your name was."

"Yes."

Rennert followed him across the hall and into his room.

"Have a chair." Fogarty extinguished the flashlight.

Rennert deposited his candle on the table and sat down. He noticed that the archaeologist glanced surreptitiously at his watch as he carried his coat and hat to the closet.

The room was similar to Weikel's and Biggerstaff's. There were a few more articles of clothing lying about, and the table was piled higher with books, papers and variegated pieces of pottery. In their midst was a typewriter, its cover in place.

Fogarty went to the table and poked about in the litter until he found a battered briar pipe and a pouch. He began to cram the bowl with tobacco, spilling a great deal on his trousers in the process. Rennert, looking past the powerful, rangy frame, could see that the pottery bore typewritten and not printed labels.

"Well—" Fogarty made an effort at joviality—"it's a bad night for the old rheumatism, isn't it? I'm beginning to feel twinges of it already."

Rennert agreed that it was an exceedingly bad night for rheumatism. "You must have gone out just in time to get caught in the rain, didn't you?"

"Yes. I was on my way to the plaza when it started." Fogarty had located a packet of matches and was moving to a chair a few feet from Rennert.

He presented a more dignified and genial figure now than he had in his work clothes. A heavy tweed coat of checkered rust and black, brown trousers and a white shirt with dark tie were in harmony with the healthy tan of the cheeks momentarily hollowed by suction. Even the incipient baldness was almost concealed by the carefully brushed iron-gray hair. It was the man's eyes, staring in fierce concentration at the match flame, which betrayed his lack of ease.

He flicked away the sliver of wax. "You wanted to see me about those skeletons, I suppose."

Without giving Rennert a chance to reply he hurried on: "I'd be glad to help you, but I'm afraid I've told you all I can. The shipment was in perfectly good order when it left here. We'll file a claim for damages with the Mexican National Railways."

"You can be of a great deal more help to me, Doctor, by answering a few questions. I assure you that they're not as irrelevant as they may sound. To begin with, you have two assistants: Karl Weikel and—what's the name of the other?"

"Biggerstaff. John Biggerstaff."

"Not Biggers?"

"Why no. Biggerstaff."

"How long have you known them?"

"I've known Karl for four years, John for three. Both of them were students of mine at Southwestern University before I resigned my position there."

"Can you tell me anything about their backgrounds?"

"Their backgrounds?" Fogarty repeated irritably, taking the pipe from his mouth. "Of what importance is that? They're both good workers and have the makings of first-rate archaeologists. That's all I'm interested in."

"I understand that. But take my word for it that you'll be acting in their own interests by answering my question."

Fogarty's teeth clamped upon the pipestem again. For some time the only sounds to break the stillness were the gurgle of saliva and the thudding of the raindrops, like spent BB shot, on the leaded panes.

"I can tell you all I know about their backgrounds in a very few words," he said abruptly. "Weikel comes from Kansas City. His father has a secondhand store or a pawnshop or something of the kind there. I don't know where Biggerstaff's home is. Both of them worked their way through college. From that I'd infer they're not rolling in wealth exactly."

"Biggerstaff attended Chicago University before going to Southwestern, didn't he?"

"He spent one term there."

"You doubtless knew Professor Garnett Voice, didn't you, Doctor?"

A frown cut into Fogarty's forehead. "Yes."

"I'd like some information about him. I thought you might be able to give it to me."

"Why yes," in a puzzled tone, "I can tell you a little about him. He spent the winter here in this house, in fact. I can't say I was particularly intimate with him. He didn't have many interests outside his own field. Rather an uninspired research worker, I always thought. A damned poor teacher. Did quite a bit of spadework on the Mexican ambitions of some of the Confederate leaders, but it'll take a man of broader intellect to make it of much real value."

"Like John Randolph's 'rotten mackerel that shines and stinks in the moonlight'?"

Fogarty chuckled. "Describes the man exactly." He sucked for a moment, contemplatively, on the pipe. "But don't tell me you suspect him of anything dishonest. I didn't mean to infer that. Intellectual dishonesty, yes, but nothing more."

"No, I'm not inquiring into his honesty, intellectual or otherwise. I understand that Weikel had some difficulty with him at Southwestern."

"Oh, so that's been dug up, has it?" Fogarty began to speak more slowly, weighing his words. "Yes. There was an altercation about a history grade. It was at the time of the annual election to Phi Beta Kappa. Weikel claimed that Voice purposely lowered his grade to keep him out. Karl's inclined to be a little hasty sometimes. I might have been able to straighten the matter out, but he went ahead and got into a row with Voice. There wasn't anything to do then. Biggerstaff was elected, but Weikel wasn't."

"Voice was a member of Phi Beta Kappa?"

"No."

"He wasn't? You're sure of that?"

"Positive. I'm a member myself, so I ought to know."

Rennert lit a cigarette and stared for a moment into its blue spirals of smoke.

"Was there any further trouble between Voice and Weikel down here?" he asked finally.

"Oh no. They seldom saw each other, except to pass in the hall."

"Nothing happened this spring to stir up Weikel's old resentment?"

Fogarty hesitated. "Why yes, come to think of it, there *was* something. Karl and John were both applying for a permanent place with the Teague Museum. There's only one open. Voice gave Biggerstaff a very good recommendation. Karl didn't even ask him for one, of course, after what had happened. He said, although I don't know whether it's true or not, that Voice had written to the museum urging them not to consider his application. Karl has a deeply ingrained inferiority complex. He's convinced that the world is against him. On account of his racial antecedents, his appearance, his poverty, any number of things. It's unfortunate, as he will always be handicapped by it."

"When did this matter of the applications come up?"

"Last April."

Rennert nodded thoughtfully. That was one of the things which had puzzled him: why an animosity of such long standing should have flared suddenly into action.

Fogarty pulled a watch from his pocket and glanced at it.

Just as he put it back into place Rennert said, "You knew about the threatening letters that Voice received?"

The other took the pipe from his mouth and sat up straighter in the chair. His *Yes* was noncommittal. "In your opinion, who wrote them?"

The long jaw moved, then set grimly. With the pipestem Fogarty described a circle in the air and jabbed accurately through its center. His eyes met Rennert's then in what was almost a glare.

"So that's it! I had the feeling that you'd been beating about the bush. I thought it odd that the United States customs authorities should send a man all the way down here to inquire into some forgeries of pottery or a damaged shipment of skeletons." He laughed. "But I'm afraid you've let yourself be led on a wild-goose chase, Mr. Rennert. I wouldn't take those letters too seriously. Someone was just pulling Voice's leg. You must know the temptation—to disturb someone's smugness? Just a schoolboy prank."

"You saw the letters, Doctor?"

"Yes."

"Did those drawings on them impress you as having been done in the spirit of a schoolboy prank?"

The archaeologist's eyes dropped, and he moved uneasily in his chair.

"Well," he admitted reluctantly, "to tell you the truth, they did worry me a bit. Whoever made them had a decidedly nasty mind, I should say."

"You would also say that the person who wrote them was inspired by a very real hatred of Voice?"

"Yes, undoubtedly."

"Enough to do murder?"

"What?" The pipe dropped from Fogarty's fingers.

"Murder, Doctor. You spoke a moment ago of beating about the bush. That's exactly what I have been doing. But to a purpose. One of the skeletons in that last shipment you sent to the border was that of Garnett Voice."

Fogarty's lips had remained parted after that last startled cry, so that the gold bridgework on his teeth gleamed in the candlelight. His tan seemed suddenly to have changed to leather, holding the facial muscles immobile.

"That's impossible," he managed. "You're insane, man, insane!"

"It's the truth, Doctor. Voice was murdered in this vicinity the first of May and his body buried in lime. Some time later it was put into a plaster cast and sent away with your specimens. That's why I'm here. The case hasn't been turned over to the Mexican authorities yet. If there's anything you have to say to me before it is, I shall be glad to hear you."

Fogarty continued to stare at him, almost blankly. The tendons of his hands stood out like tightened wires as he grasped the chair arms.

"Before God, Rennert, what I told you this afternoon was the truth! I can see no possible way this could have happened."

"Remember the forged pottery on your previous shipment. The two substitutions could only have been the work of someone familiar with your excavations. The list is limited. Biggerstaff, Weikel—"

"No, no!" Fogarty started to his feet and began to stalk with long strides, his hands jammed into his pockets. "You've led me on to talk about my assistants. But they couldn't have done this. Their whole future is bound up with our work here. They wouldn't have had anything to gain."

"What about the original pottery and the skeleton that disappeared? Wouldn't they have some value?"

Fogarty stopped. "Yes, that's right. They were valuable. Any museum would be glad to get hold of them."

"I thought so. There's one more person to consider. Diego Echave, the inspector for the Department of Archaeology."

The archaeologist stood towering over the candle, his gaze fixed on it as if in fascination.

"Echave," he repeated slowly.

Rennert sat half shadowed by the tall body and watched conflicting emotions play across the sharp features.

"There is going to be a very close inquiry into the management of your expedition, Dr. Fogarty. Questions are going to be asked about the share the Mexican government has got out of these finds. The reports which Echave has turned in are going to be inspected carefully. Do you know a man by the name of Moises Sart, who lives on the Paseo de la Reforma?"

"Sart? Why, of course. He has a large collection of Mexican antiquities. That is, he's supposed to have. Very few have ever seen them. He used to do some digging himself, I believe, but in recent years he has left the work to agents. Why?"

"I thought you might be interested in knowing that your friend Echave paid a hurried call to his house on leaving you tonight. After learning that I was suspicious about your shipments."

Fogarty's fist struck the palm of his hand. "He did, did he? To Sart, whose Archaic collection is said to be so good."

He took a deep breath and expelled it noisily. He moved back to the chair like a man in a daze and sank into it heavily. He bent forward and raised one hand to wrinkle the skin of his forehead.

His voice sounded deflated. "You win, Mr. Rennert. I can see I'm in a tight spot. I'm not going to try to excuse myself by saying that I've only done what my competitors have been doing for years. The Teague Museum is a new one and entered the Mexican field after the Eastern museums were already entrenched. We wanted to enlarge our collection as quickly as possible, so when Echave approached me at the beginning of the season with regard to . . . an arrangement between ourselves, I agreed. Not without a qualm of conscience, I admit, but I agreed. For a small sum I was to be allowed to take out of the country whatever I wanted of our finds. He turned the rest over to the government and reported that this was the full share due them."

He cleared his throat and said earnestly, "No one knew of this except the two of us. Weikel and Biggerstaff did *not*. Get that straight. It worked satisfactorily until—" anger underscored the words—"Echave began to raise the price above that agreed on. I protested, but there was nothing I could do. If I reported him to his superiors it would only mean that I'd get into trouble and lose material that I wanted badly. I can see now that he's been double-crossing me, collecting from me for permission to send the stuff out, then stealing it and selling it to Sart. You probably won't understand, Rennert, what a temptation it was to me. We were speaking a moment ago about honesty, intellectual and material. Voice would never have done what I did. *But* he would have suppressed a manuscript that conflicted with some thesis he was building up. I wouldn't. That was the difference between us. But there— I said I wasn't going to try to exculpate myself."

"Thank you, Doctor. You'll find that you have acted wisely in telling me this. Now I want you to write out a complete statement of what you have just told me. You have a typewriter there, I see. List every object, as far as you can, which you sent out of Mexico this winter."

"What has already been sent away—can that be confiscated?"

"As to that, I can't say. I think, however, that the Mexican government will be disposed to leniency in return for your testimony against Echave. He has probably been engaged in the same operation with other expeditions. In the meantime I'll take your place in the interview with Echave. At nine, isn't it?"

"So you know about that. Yes, it's at nine."

"May I borrow your flashlight?"

"Certainly."

Fogarty got up and moved to the chair by the table. He took the cover from the typewriter and slipped a sheet of paper into the machine.

"This is really a death warrant that I'm going to type, isn't it?" he said.

"A death warrant?"

"Yes, for Echave. If it had been anything but murder I might condone it."

Rennert watched the long, big-knuckled fingers poise above the keys.

"What motive," he asked, "would you give for Echave's murder of Voice?"

Fogarty looked up, startled. "Motive? Why, I haven't thought of that."

"Abandoned cemeteries are common enough here in Mexico, had he merely wanted a skeleton."

The room was very still for a moment, and Fogarty's laugh was incongruously loud. "Oh, it's easy enough to find a motive. Voice may have got wise to his graft and Echave had to kill him to keep him from talking. It's likely that money was involved, isn't it?"

"Yes," Rennert said abstractedly, "it is."

The clicking of the keys was in his ears as he went down the hall. He secured his hat and raincoat from the stand and made his way across the landing to the rear door.

The rain still descended in a steady downpour, obscuring his vision. His feet slipped in the shifting gravel and mud as they followed the course of the wavering cone of light toward the coach house. It was bitterly cold.

He came at last, wet and tired, to the doors. Sliding them back on their grooves, he stepped inside and closed them behind him. He sent the beam of the torch darting about the room until he had ascertained that there was no one there. No one, at least, who wanted to make his presence known.

He began a slow circuit of the place, his senses alert. A rat scurried for cover behind some loose sacking. The rain beat monotonously on the shingled roof.

He came to the trestle table, where they had stood that afternoon. He leaned upon it and waited.

The light traveled here and there, idly, over the dusty floor. It rested for an instant on a burlap bag which lay in the center of the room. It started to move on, then came back with a jerk.

Rennert moved swiftly forward and knelt upon the bricks. Carefully he threw back the bag, through whose porous sides moisture had seeped.

The torch's rays glistened upon the dark pool beneath.

He got up and directed the light in a circle about him. Little drops, like those of discolored rain, had spattered the dust toward the southeast corner.

He followed them unerringly to a pile of broken packing cases. He began to throw the splintered wood aside.

It was a matter of seconds only before he stopped, let fall the board which he had raised and bent over what it had concealed.

In other circumstances recognition might have been slow in coming.

On account of the blood. It matted the dark hair and covered the face, which was twisted at an unnatural angle toward one shoulder. The left temple was a sickening, clotted mass about a gaping hole.

It was Diego Echave.

Tossed upon his body, like an ironic crucifix, was a double-edged pick.

21
KEY

RENNERT STRAIGHTENED UP and surveyed his fingertips with eyes bleakened by repugnance.

The blood was still warm.

He shoved open one of the doors and held his right hand out into the rain.

The rain which had washed away betraying footprints, he reflected, as his left hand swept the torch in a widening semicircle over the dark rivulets of water cutting their channels through the soft earth. Even his own prints were almost gone.

He dried his hand with his handkerchief and lit a cigarette. He smoked and stared into the rain-filled night.

It was impossible now to keep the police out of the affair. In no other land, probably, does a corpse assume *per se* as much importance as in Mexico. Transgressions against a living man may be regarded as mitigated by a multitude of considerations. But once he is dead—irrevocably and demonstrably dead—he becomes, as it were, sacrosanct. In Mexico dying is man's most significant act. By the mere touching of the lifeless body in that corner Rennert had put himself in imperative need of a dispensation which could come only from certain high quarters in Mexico City.

He started up the incline toward the house.

Pieces of the puzzle were falling into place now, with a neatness in which he felt a purely impersonal pleasure. They required only the final welding of proof. And, he realized wearily, there was little enough of that.

But wasn't there?

The thought brought him to an abrupt stop.

He turned and walked with quickened step back to the coach house.

He strode across the room and located a spade. With it thrown over his shoulder he went again into the night.

Fitting, he thought, that a skeleton should finish what a skeleton had begun. . . .

It was fully fifteen minutes before he got to his feet and began to throw the viscous black mud back into the shallow hole.

When it was filled he trod upon it. The flashlight, propped up on a stone, illuminated his muddy shoes, the sodden cuffs of his trousers and the splattered hem of his raincoat. It left in shadow the grimace of distaste which hardened his nostrils and lips.

He returned the spade to its place, then directed his steps toward the house, breathing deeply of the clean, cold air.

Having no key to the rear door, he let himself in at the front.

The muffled click of the typewriter keys greeted him as he tramped up the stairs and down the hall to Fogarty's room.

The archaeologist looked up in surprise as he entered. He had his pipe going again, and the room was filled with the pungent odor of tobacco.

"Hullo, Rennert. Didn't expect you back so soon. Didn't Echave show up?"

"Yes, he showed up. A little prior to the time you and he agreed on." Rennert disregarded the question in the other's eyes. "You mentioned the fact that you were a Phi Beta Kappa, Doctor. Do you have your key?"

Fogarty's wide lips, chapped and hardened by wind and sun, always seemed to move into a laugh with difficulty.

"My key? Lord, no. Don't have the faintest idea where it is. I never wear it more than once or twice a year. Too ostentatious."

"You didn't bring it to Mexico, then?"

"No. It wouldn't be of any use to me down here. I left it back in San Antonio."

"Of course. Do you know whether John Biggerstaff has one?"

"Yes. The novelty of it hasn't quite worn off for him yet."

"I'll leave you now, Doctor, while you finish your statement." Rennert extended a hand.

Fogarty, obviously surprised at the gesture, took it with lax fingers. His expression changed abruptly to one of astonishment. "I didn't know that."

Rennert smiled. "I didn't see any need to tell you before."

"Testing my veracity, were you?"

"No, Doctor, testing my own memory. Good-by."

Rennert walked down the hall to Biggerstaff's room. He entered quietly, keeping the light directed away from the bed. He glanced in that direction, however, and saw that it was empty.

On the little table near the head were the box of sedative tablets and an empty glass. The glass which Biggerstaff had had at his lips as he and Roark went out.

For a full minute Rennert centered the light upon the pillow, which still retained the impress of the young man's head. He was frowning.

The frown cleared, and he moved to the improvised closet. With nimble fingers he went through the clothing which hung there.

Next he had recourse to the dresser. In one of the top drawers he found the little square key, stemming at the top into a ring, which abrasion might well wear off. Knobs, Monica had called them, at top and bottom.

He held it to the light, and for an instant his thoughts strayed as he studied the once-familiar design. On one side, the three bold Greek letters and the hand directing man's arduous journey to the stars. On the reverse, the name John Clay Biggerstaff, faintly inscribed, the intertwined initials and the date, December 5, 1776. Usage had taken off its brightness and scratches had marred its surface, but it still gave back the light of the torch.

What a grim jest it was, he thought as he slipped the key into a vest pocket, that such a relic of the gray halls of learning should play a part in another episode of Mexico's blood-drenched soil.

It was as he was closing the drawer that the sight of the newspaper in the bottom started another train of thought. Why not? The supposed note from Voice had come on the second of May. On that day or soon afterwards his belongings would have been packed and removed to the coach house. An occasion, if he had any knowledge of feminine housekeeping, for a renovation of the vacated quarters. . . .

But that would have to wait.

Rennert left the room and went down the rear stairs to the kitchen.

It was the first time he had visited this part of the house, and he cast a swift, interested glance about the room. The walls above a charcoal stove were grimy from smoke, and the curtains at the windows were frayed. But a meticulous hand had seen that the tiled floor was clean and that the rows of utensils could flash back the light of his torch.

There was a table in the center of the room and on it a candle. Across the unflickering flame Marta was looking at him.

Seen thus, with the light lengthening and softening her dark face and glittering back from her eyes, she belied the prosaic background. The ugly factory-made dress loosened and accommodated itself with an unstudied grace to her lithe, full body. The bracelet gleamed bright and barbaric.

Rennert closed the door and came closer. "Marta, you know that I am a guest in the house, that Miss Faudree has given me permission to ask questions?"

She nodded.

"I want to know if anyone besides yourself has been in this kitchen tonight, during or since dinner?"

"No sir. No one has been." Her voice was low and not unmelodious, but again he detected that lack of precision in her enunciation. Her English, evidently acquired in this house, was a curious echo of Lucy's speech.

"The door to the rear hall has been closed?"

"Yes sir."

"Do you know what people have been in or out of it?"

Her head moved back and forth in a negative, which she reinforced with a toneless "No."

"Have you seen Diego Echave tonight?"

Something stirred deep in her eyes, but they did not waver. "No sir. I have not seen him."

"Someone killed him tonight, Marta, in the coach house."

Rennert, watching her face, saw the emotional unrestraint which was a heritage of one of her forbears struggling with the impassivity of the other. She crossed herself quickly, and her lips moved without sound. He speculated briefly what the man might have meant to her.

He went on: "The person who killed him took from his neck a piece of gold on a thong. You have seen it?"

"Yes sir."

Rennert extended a palm on which lay Biggerstaff's Phi Beta Kappa key. "Was it like this Marta?"

She stared down, the lids of her eyes dropping slightly. She nodded. "Yes sir."

He turned the key over and put a fingernail upon the two lines at the top. "Was there a name here, Marta?"

"I do not know. It was dirty. The letters were not plain."

As he had thought. Those diminutive lines which, in this case, were all-important would be the first to fade with abrasion.

He replaced the key in his pocket and asked: "Señor Echave found this in the gully north of the coach house, didn't he?"

"Yes sir."

"Did anyone besides yourself know that he found it?" He saw her hesitate and added, "And Monica Faudree."

"No sir," she said then, readily.

"Did Echave ever find anything else in this gully, Marta?"

She thought for a moment, running the bracelet up and down her arm with long, flexible fingers. "There were some old bones," she said.

The little globules of wax tumbled down the sides of the candle, hissing faintly and sending their odor to Rennert's nostrils. The excitement in his eyes made them almost as bright as hers.

"Echave found the bones where he found this piece of gold?"

"I saw them there. I showed them to him."

"When?"

She was entirely Mexican in her vagueness. "A long time ago."

"About the time the summer rains started?"

"Yes." She grasped at this. "When the rains started."

He regarded her for a moment, debating whether to venture further along a line of inquiry of whose goal he was already certain.

"Did Echave come at night to the coach house," he asked, "to the old stables where the archaeologists work?"

There was no expression at all on her face or in her eyes now. "Sometimes."

"Do you know why he came?"

"I do not know," she replied simply.

Although the motion was invisible, he saw the effect of the tightening of her facial muscles. He knew the futility of proceeding where a negative would be so easily given and so unassailable.

"Marta," he said, "the body of Diego Echave is still out in the coach house. We must call the police and a doctor. Are you willing to go up to the plaza to a telephone?" He laid a bill on the table.

She scarcely glanced at it. "Yes sir."

"Very well. You are to call this number in Mexico City. You are to ask for Lieutenant Jaime Tresguerras." He wrote on a slip of paper. "Tell him to come here immediately, if it is possible, and. bring a doctor with him. I shall meet him in the coach house. Is that clear?"

"Yes sir."

He started away, then turned. "You remember Professor Voice?"

"Voice?" she repeated. "Yes, I remember."

"He used to live in the southeast room upstairs. The one I have now. Did you clean that room after he left?"

"Yes sir."

"Did you put newspapers in the drawers of the wardrobe?"

She nodded. "Yes sir."

"Thank you, Marta."

There were other means of verifying that theory of his, he reflected as he went up the stairs. But this was quicker.

In his room, he went directly to the wardrobe and removed one of the drawers below the glass panels. He emptied onto the bed the clothing which he had put into place such a short time before. The newspaper in the bottom was the Mexico City *Excelsior* of May 2.

These were the front and back pages of the first section. He ran his eyes over them hastily, then thrust them back.

He followed the same procedure with the other drawer. On the second page he found what he was seeking. He sank on the bed, recklessly crushing shirts, and held the flashlight to the printed sheet as with the other hand he took from his pocket the envelope which he had found in Voice's coat.

His eyes went from the numbers on the envelope to those in the newspaper. A3,400. A3,401. A3,402. . . .

Nothing there.

He went on to the next column. G735. G736. . . .

It was not until he came to P22,007, in the last column, that he let the newspaper fall on the bed.

He knew why Garnett Voice had been killed.

He drew a breath of relief that the motive was such a simple one.

22
LIE

THE RAIN MUST HAVE been slackening for several minutes before Rennert was brought to awareness of the fact by sounds which reached him from the length of the hall. Low voices, a man's laughter, the shutting of a door.

He had his own door open in time to see the glimmer of candlelight blotted out by the closing of Biggerstaff's.

He went back to the bed, tore from the newspaper the section which interested him and put it and the envelope into his coat pocket.

That pocket would have bulged had its contents possessed size relative to their importance. He enumerated them as he went down the hall:

The two extortion letters and the letter of credentials which he had brought from the embassy.

Two empty envelopes, one bearing a specimen of typing from Voice's machine, the other the series of numbers.

The scrap of newspaper which explained those numbers.

He came to Monica's door and knocked. When Cornell opened it and let him enter, he commented mentally upon the fact that it had not been locked.

"Was that you who went out to the coach house a few minutes ago, Mr. Rennert?" she asked as soon as he was inside.

"Yes."

"I saw the light. I wondered if anything was wrong."

149

"There was, Miss Faudree. Diego Echave, the Mexican inspector, was murdered there tonight."

"Echave!" She covered her face with her hands, and a shudder went through her. "Oh, isn't this ever going to end, Mr. Rennert?"

"I think the end is near now."

She lowered her hands suddenly, to expose a face gone white and rigid. "What time was Echave killed?"

"Sometime between eight and nine, I believe."

"Do you know who killed him?"

"I have no proof yet." Rennert was confirming the suspicion which he had had when he entered—that there was a faint bluish haze of cigarette smoke in the air.

She must have observed this, for she turned hastily and went to the window. She opened the lower sash several inches.

"It's stuffy in here, isn't it?" she said as she came back. Then, without a pause, "Monica's all right now. I think we'd better let her sleep until morning."

Rennert looked at the bed, from which came a thin, regular snore. Indeed the woman seemed, to all appearances, sunk into a deep and natural slumber.

"Has she wakened?" he asked.

"No." She spoke jerkily, as if her thoughts were elsewhere. "But I know there's nothing wrong with her."

"How do you account for her sudden sleepiness then?"

She looked away. "I think she took a sleeping powder."

He regarded her for a moment in silence.

"Did she have sleeping powders here?"

"I—I suppose so," she faltered.

"Or did she take one of John Biggerstaff's?" he asked quietly.

Her laugh was indecorously loud in that room whose stillness was broken only by the snoring and a drip from the gutter which struck the window ledge at regularly spaced intervals.

Her eyes met his levelly. "Mr. Rennert, it's nonsense—our talking at cross purposes in this way. Please take my word about John, won't you?"

His smile was pleasant. "I'll be inclined to if you will answer my question."

"Very well, I *will* answer it. She took one of John's powders."

"By accident?"

"Yes." The girl was a poor prevaricator. Her eyes fell and darted, as nearly as he could tell, from his chin to the knot of his tie, to the top button of his vest, then back. "You see," she went on hurriedly, "I got one of those tablets from John's room. I felt nervous, didn't think I could sleep tonight. I had it in my room, in a glass of water. Monica came up and drank it without knowing what it was. That's all."

"Simple enough," he said kindly. "Thank you."

"Yes." She was in haste to change the subject. "Where's Delaney?"

"He went back to Mexico City."

"You gave him my message?"

"Yes. This is what he said: 'Tell Cornell she's better off not seeing me any more.'"

She turned her head so that her eyes were in shadow.

"I'm sorry he feels that way," she said in a low voice. "He shouldn't. Do you know Delaney very well, Mr. Rennert?"

"I only met him this afternoon."

"Then you don't know about his life nowadays?"

"No." Rennert was interested. "He has your picture in his office."

Her eyes were troubled as they came back to his face. "He has?"

"Yes, I saw it before I saw you. In fact it was the second I had seen. John Biggerstaff carries one in his billfold."

"That snapshot!" She laughed weakly. "I didn't know he'd kept it. I didn't know that Delaney had kept my picture either. It was an old one, wasn't it?"

"So I would judge."

Her eyes almost closed, and her voice, when it came, was soft and meditative:

"It seems such an incredibly long time since I gave Delaney that. In another life almost. It's hard to believe it was less than ten years ago and that I was so foolish. It was after the Revolution was definitely over, and things had settled down, so that we could see what the fighting had been about. What the bloodshed and the suffering had accomplished. I suppose it's the same after every war. My grandfather got the aftermath of one. He came to Mexico because he couldn't adjust himself when it was finished. You felt the same disillusionment in the United States after your last war, I know. The same bitterness toward the ideals that you'd waved flags for. The same hectic efforts to keep from having ideals. The same facile talk about self-expression and all that."

She paused. "Mr. Rennert, do you understand what I'm trying to say?"

"I understand very well."

"We didn't have another country to escape to, like my grandfather. And it was easier for us to go the full length of the wave. Everything's done by extremes in Mexico. I was attending art school in Mexico City then. Not very conscientiously, but because Lucy thought a girl ought to be exposed to that sort of thing in order to become a lady. I was rather at loose ends, so I got caught up with a young crowd like myself. Delaney was one of us. He had just come back from college in the United States. He had all the highest honors the school could give and a brilliant future. My memories of those days are mostly vague. Rooms stuffy with cigarette smoke and alcohol. People sitting around on the floor. Somebody half drunk and reading French poetry. A phonograph blaring out American jazz."

She squared her shoulders. "I snapped out of it pretty quickly. With a feeling of disgust. Not for the people I'd been associated with—although I seldom have seen any of them again—but for the senselessness of the whole thing. It may have been my own common sense or merely a weak constitution, I don't know. It didn't hurt me any. I didn't even learn to smoke during the orgy. A sort of declaration of my solitary independence. That's why Delaney acted the way he did this afternoon with those cigarettes. Poor Delaney, I'm afraid he hasn't recovered from those years. This is the first time I've seen him lately, but from what I've heard he's still living that life. Keeping head over heels in debt, ruining his prospects for a career. I thought I'd like to see him again; show him that I don't blame him for anything."

She was silent for a moment, staring past Rennert at the low three-tiered bookcase, on top of which rested a white sea shell.

"Maybe you'll understand now, Mr. Rennert, why meeting John meant so much to me. He's so clean and healthy and—well, I suppose wholesome is the only word. I know I'll always be safe with him."

Rennert moved slightly, and his gaze fell, quite naturally, on the shell. In it lay a crushed cigarette stub, from which still coiled a tiny thread of smoke.

Cornell's teeth sank into her lip. She looked up at him and saw that he had noticed it.

Her laugh was brittle. "You can see I wasn't telling the truth about cigarettes, Mr. Rennert. I *do* smoke."

Rennert regretted afterward what he did then. He took out a package and offered her one.

She took it without hesitation, inserted it in the center of her lips and held it up to the match which he struck.

"I don't know why I've been talking away to you like this." She spoke indistinctly, the white tube wavering. "Baring my life to you while Monica snores peacefully away."

He was watching her as smoke began to curtain her face. "I'm glad you have, Miss Faudree. You've told me several things I wanted to know."

"Have I? I—" The words were choked off by a paroxysm of coughing.

Rennert was at her side instantly, removing the cigarette from her fingers.

"That was cruel of me," he said sternly as he crushed it out. "I ought to be kicked for calling your bluff."

She was gasping as her eyes blinked to force back the tears. "I'm all right. I just choked."

"I know," he said. "Shall we say good night on that?"

She nodded and preceded him from the room. By the time he had extinguished the guttering candle she had closed her door.

He crossed at once to Biggerstaff's room. This time he did not dim the light.

The young man lay in the bed, eyes closed and one hand on his chest. His breathing came faintly and irregularly.

Rennert pulled up a chair and sat down, the flashlight resting on his knee.

For perhaps two minutes he sat there, his watch ticking dispassionately in the stillness.

Then Biggerstaff said, "I'm not asleep."

Rennert said, "I know you're not."

23
NAME

BIGGERSTAFF RAISED his head and wadded a pillow beneath it.

"How did you know?" he asked.

Rennert held the light so that it illuminated the bandaged hand and the hump of bedclothes that was the young man's chest.

"I came in here and found you gone. Do you mind being told that you were a damned fool—in more ways than one?"

"Not at all," was the cheerful reply. "I know it."

"I've just come from Monica's room."

"Cornell still there?"

"She left a moment ago."

"I suppose she told you about the sedative?"

"She told me her version. Let's hear yours."

"I'm awfully sorry it happened. I didn't know about it till it was too late. It didn't hurt Monica, did it?"

"No. It enabled someone to hide in her room and make way with a letter which would have helped me. That's all."

"Oh say, Mr. Rennert—I'm sorry."

"It can't be helped now. Tell me how it happened. No, keep that head down."

"All right." Biggerstaff obeyed. "Well, Monica came in here just after you and Mr. Roark left. I hadn't drunk the sedative. I thought I'd get a short nap, then see Cornell. I wanted to talk to her alone for a few minutes. So I left the glass there on the table. Monica sat where you're sitting. Looked at me and—and brushed my forehead a little." He seemed embarrassed. "I kept my eyes closed and

155

pretended I was asleep. I thought she'd go. But she didn't. She stayed for about an hour, until the dinner chimes rang. Then I saw that she had drunk that water with the sedative in it. I started to call her back, but I knew it wouldn't hurt her." His lips parted in a wide grin, so that his teeth gleamed whitely against his dark skin. "I thought it was a rather good joke on her."

"Then you went to Cornell's apartment?"

"Yes."

"And when I called her to Monica's room you followed her down?"

"Yes. I felt to blame, you see."

Biggerstaff was silent for several seconds, his eyes fixed on the fingers of his left hand, which moved spiderlike over the covers, supporting their tiny crests of dark hair.

"Were you ever in love, Mr. Rennert?" he asked finally, in a serious, confidential voice.

Rennert kept his face sober. He knew that the question required no answer.

"Well, I am," Biggerstaff announced.

"I judged that," Rennert said.

"It's the only thing that makes life worth while, Mr. Rennert." The young voice was magisterial. "But . . . it makes it awfully hard sometimes, too."

Rennert watched the intent face and thought of the things one couldn't put into words: the lotus flower out of which the pages of some books are made; the fellowship of the sawdust floor; the warming ecstasy which comes when a man chances upon a place where, instantly, he knows that he belongs, as if in another existence his feet had walked there. Things constant and compatible only with a free if solitary body. Futile and unkind to try to explain them to this youngster, who was continuing:

"You see, Mr. Rennert, it's the question of money. I hadn't realized how important that was going to be. Cornell and I—well, we've been sort of engaged for a long time. We didn't say anything about it because of—well, because of her aunt Lucy. Lucy never seemed to like me very much."

"Although you tried to pretend you were from the South?"

"Yes. I suppose I didn't do that very well. I thought that if I said 'you-all' and dropped my *rs* and told her I was of a Confederate family she'd think it all right for Cornell to marry me. Of course we were going to be married anyway, when I got a permanent job, but I thought it'd be better if family relations were congenial for Cornell. Well, when I got back here I found this letter from the museum, saying I had the job. I thought everything was fixed then. That Cornell and I could be married right away and live in San Antonio. That's why I went up to see her tonight. To ask her. She told me just what the situation here is. Lucy and Monica don't have any money. Cornell herself didn't realize until lately just how hard up they are. They've sold all the valuable old furniture and substituted cheap imitations. Why, they don't even have money enough . . ." He hesitated.

"To pay the light and telephone bills?" Rennert supplied.

"Yes. The arrangement is to divide up the household expenses. Lucy is supposed to pay for the lights, Monica for the telephone and Cornell for the water. Well, this is the second month the other bills haven't been paid. Last month Lucy pretended that she'd forgotten. Cornell went ahead and paid them without saying anything. But now it's happened again. And Cornell says she can't go off to the United States and leave them here helpless. She doesn't have any money of her own, but can always rent rooms or get a job. If I only had enough to support all three of them it'd be different. But I don't. I only have this job with the museum, and it'll be years before I have enough to support two establishments. And in the meantime there's nothing to do but wait, with a thousand miles between us."

Rennert waited. His suspicions about several things had been confirmed: the furniture in the parlor, the inopportune failure of the lights and telephone. He thought of Lucy's elaborate casualness over the food and wine supplied for his benefit at dinner.

"There's an alternative," Biggerstaff said, very low. He turned in the bed so that he faced Rennert. "Mr. Rennert, I want to ask your advice. Do you object?"

"Not at all. I thought you had something else on your mind."

Biggerstaff started to raise himself up on an elbow. "May I get a cigarette? I've got some in my dressing gown."

"Here's one." Rennert supplied him.

The young man lay back, slowly inhaling smoke. "My name isn't Biggerstaff," he said.

"It's Biggers, isn't it?"

"Yes. How did you know? Did Karl tell you?"

"No." Rennert told him of the additional syllable stamped on the billfold and of the transcript of credits at Southwestern University.

Biggerstaff listened, frowning. "You must have thought I was a suspicious character. A man with a past."

"I admit I wondered about you. Know the old song of the Southwest? 'What was your name back in the States?'"

"Well, I'm something like those fellows who came to a new country. My name's Biggers, all right. My father's T. J. Biggers, of Chicago. I don't know whether you've ever heard of him or not, but he's a rather important banker. We were one of the first families there. Dad owns a lot of property in the Loop district and's on the boards of a lot of corporations and civic committees. Mother's one of the patrons of the Chicago Civic Opera. The society columns keep her picture set up. You know, all that sort of thing."

He dismissed it with an airy wave of the hand and was silent for a moment, a reminiscent smile playing about his lips.

"You're probably expecting to learn that I'm the disinherited son. It's not that. Somewhat of a black sheep, but nothing more. Did you ever read Jack London's *Star Rover*, Mr. Rennert?"

"Yes."

"Well, that book made a hell of an impression on me when I was a kid. I've often tried to imagine that I could relive another incarnation. I've picked out periods of history I'd like to 've lived in, the kind of person I'd like to have been. My favorite is one of Cortez' soldiers. A young fellow who was disgusted with court life in Spain, where everyone was born to a certain rank and where life was regulated by convention. I've imagined myself throwing all this up and sailing to a new world, where one man was as good as another as long as he had a good sword arm. That's how I used to feel. I was fed up with having my life laid out for me, with being told what people I could know and what I could study in school. I was supposed to go into a bank of my father's in Chicago. No one thought of asking me whether I wanted to be a banker or not. The men of our family have always been, so that was that. But I thought different. I wanted to do something else, I didn't know just what. I'd always been fascinated by archaeology, so after I finished prep school I told my father I wanted to study archaeology and not banking."

He reached out to knock the ash from his cigarette. "But, hell, I'm boring you with all this, Mr. Rennert."

"Not at all," Rennert said, in much the same tone he had used with Cornell. "You're telling me a lot of things I want to know. Go ahead."

"Well, Dad didn't take me very seriously. I suppose he thought it was just a passing fancy. He told me to go ahead. I went to the University of Chicago one term. I found, though, that I hadn't really got away from the Biggers name and money. Everyone treated me like a millionaire playboy who wanted something to amuse himself with until he got a degree. I made good grades, but the other students acted as if they thought I was getting them because the profs knew who I was. I overheard a remark once, that I was being carried through in archaeology because the members of the department thought they could induce Dad to put some money into research. Well, that first summer I tried to get a job with an expedition that was going out from the university. Everybody was very nice, but I didn't get it. They told me it'd be hard work and uninteresting. There was the feeling, too, that jobs ought to go to students who needed the money. I was pretty discouraged over the prospect. Then, at the beginning of the fall term, my father asked me if I wasn't ready to quit playing with archaeology and take up banking for good. I sort of lost my temper. I told him I was going off to some university at a distance, where no one would know who I was, and become an archaeologist. He couldn't understand my point of view, but he took it very well. He said I could go anywhere

I wanted to, that my allowance would go on just the same. I said I didn't want any allowance. I had enough saved up to put me through the university, plus what I could earn in the summers. So I went to Southwestern. I just added 'taff' to 'Biggers' and had a new name. It was easy. Then I got this job. And no one—" there was triumph in his voice—"ever knew who I was. No one has been able to accuse me of having things made easier for me because my father has money."

"Except Karl Weikel," Rennert said quietly. Biggerstaff's fingers mangled the cigarette upon the tray as if he were venting his feelings.

"Yes. Karl found out some way. That was our last year in college. He tried to borrow some money from me. When I told him I didn't have it he called me a liar. Said he knew who my father was. I tried to explain that I wasn't getting any money from home, and why, but he didn't believe me. He made some rather nasty remarks about my being a capitalist and taking the bread out of working people's mouths. That's why he said what he did this afternoon when I told him about my job."

"So that you owe the job only to your record at Southwestern?"

"Exactly."

"Phi Beta Kappa, among other things?"

"Well, yes. I am a Phi Bete. I suppose that helped."

"And it was fairly certain, when you and Weikel put in your applications this spring, that the place would go to you?"

"Yes, I think it was. What are you driving at?"

"This: That Phi Beta Kappa election, when you were chosen and Weikel wasn't, proved this spring to be a turning point in both your lives. Weikel blamed Professor Voice—rightly or wrongly doesn't matter—for his failure."

The young man seemed bothered. His fingers plucked at the edge of the sheet. "Yes, I think you can put it that way. Mr. Rennert, what have you done about Karl?"

"I'm going to have another talk with him in a few minutes." Rennert glanced at his watch. A car would be speeding now, on its way from the capital.

Biggerstaff asked, "Can you wait just a moment longer, Mr. Rennert? I haven't really put my problem to you. I can write to my father and tell him I've decided to give up archaeology and come home to the bank. Cornell and I can be married and—" he laughed bitterly—"spend the rest of our lives moving in the best social circles. I suppose that's the thing to do, although it's hard as hell just when I've got the job I've been wanting so long."

"You have never told Cornell of this?"

"No." Biggerstaff turned away. "I've been afraid that she'd want me to choose Chicago. That even if she didn't say so, she'd always blame me for all the things she couldn't have on my small salary at the museum. I know I'm being unjust to her—but I've been afraid, that's all. Mr. Rennert, what would you do?"

Rennert rose and took the empty glass from the table. "The Mexicans have a saying which covers the problem exactly, Biggerstaff. 'Tomorrow is another day.' I'll give you one bit of advice right now. Tell Cornell. She's a brave girl. She made a heroic sacrifice for you tonight."

"A sacrifice?" Biggerstaff glanced up at him quickly. "What do you mean?"

"The whereabouts of everyone between eight and nine tonight have become very important. I'll tell you why tomorrow. When she learned that, she tried to hide from me the fact that you had been out of your room during that time. She told me that the cigarette stub in Monica's room was hers. She even tried to smoke a cigarette to prove it. Now, young man, I'm going to stand over you until this sedative is down your throat."

Rennert went into the bathroom, filled the glass with water and dropped in two of the tablets. He gave it to Biggerstaff and watched him swallow it, then lie back with a wry face.

"Now," he said as he took the glass, "both you and Monica are disposed of for the night. Hasta mañana." He extended a hand, his left.

Biggerstaff took it eagerly. His palm was as large as and much rougher than Rennert's.

"Thanks, Mr. Rennert. I'll repay you sometime—" He stopped, and his jaw fell slightly. "Well, I'll be damned," he said slowly. "Why didn't you tell me?"

"This is the first occasion I've had." Rennert withdrew his hand.

"Is that the reason you've been so interested in me?"

Deliberately Rennert prevaricated. "Yes."

"Well, thanks." Biggerstaff laughed. "But nothing short of finding a hidden treasure is going to help Cornell and me."

Rennert stared at him for a moment.

"Strange," he said, "that you should say that."

24
PROOF

"WELL?" RENNERT SAID on the threshold of Weikel's room.

The candle there had burned very low, and a thin pencil of smoke rose from the shriveled wick which protruded from the wax. The weakening rays shifted and flickered over the heavy, fleshy face of the young man who sat slumped in the chair, hands clasped between his knees.

Rennert's keen eyes took tally of the bedroom slippers on the big feet planted squarely on the floor, the dry, dusty boots in the angle between the bed and the closet, the threadbare Brussels carpet unstreaked by moisture.

He said, "Since I left you, Diego Echave has been found murdered in the coach house. The police are on their way here from Mexico City. You have perhaps ten minutes to say things to me."

Weikel gripped his hands together so tightly that, sun-darkened as they were, the knuckles stood out white.

"What do you want to know?" Rennert noted the change in his voice. Most of its gruffness was gone, replaced by a plaintive, defensive note.

"I want you to tell me about the letters which were sent to Professor Voice and about the owls which hooted at his window."

Half a minute went by.

A spasmodic twitching went over Weikel's face. It passed, and he spoke in a sudden, almost incoherent outburst:

"All right. I'll tell you. . . ."

Perhaps five of those minutes had gone when two cars chugged through the mud of the lane and came to a stop in front of the house.

"That will do, Weikel," Rennert said. "I think this is the police."

Weikel raised his tiny bleared eyes. "What are you going to do? Send me to jail?"

Rennert regarded him for a moment. Gone now was most of his antipathy toward this young man who, not altogether by his own fault, had damned himself so long and so miserably. He remembered his words to Roark that afternoon, that the trail of the letters would lead to a person in some kind of prison. The cell between whose narrow walls Weikel paced was likely to be as loathsome as those of Ulúa. Certainly it had bred as ugly things.

He said at the door, "No, I'm not going to send you to jail, Weikel. A psychiatric clinic is the place for you."

It was the best he could do.

Once again he was walking down that long silent hall, descending the carpeted treads to the landing, crossing this to the measured tick of the clock below, going down the steep flight to the rear door. Every inch of that route was familiar to him now. He knew where the boards creaked, where there were rents in the dark, flowered wallpaper, and where seeping moisture had left paler bloated spots.

The rain had diminished to a fine drizzle when he stepped on the spongy grass. It was piercingly cold as he waited at the foot of the old cedar tree, his light playing about its base until voices and the flashes of a torch told him that the newcomers were turning the side of the house and advancing in the direction of the coach house.

He met them at the doors, his light playing briefly upon two stolid dark-visaged policemen in uniform, an elderly man who carried a black case, and coming to rest upon the face of Lieutenant Tresguerras.

At first glance Jaime Heliodoro Tresguerras seemed scarcely worthy of such a resounding and bellicose name. He was of slight, almost delicate build, with a certain effeteness of manner. This was offset by the strong strain of Indian blood which manifested itself in the high cheekbones, the straight jet-black hair, the still expressionless eyes with their deceptive aspect of Buddhalike introspection. Rennert had known many men who had been thrown off their guard by the harmless exterior, so that they had forgotten to watch those eyes.

The Mexican's electric torch must have revealed some of the emotional strain under which Rennert had been laboring, for the latter felt the black eyes boring into his as they shook hands.

"So we meet another time, Señor Rennert! And it must be death which brings us together."

"That pleasure," Rennert said, "takes some of the ugliness from death." He glanced at the man who had paused on the threshold and at the two policemen who had planted themselves, atlantean, on either side of the doorway.

"This," Tresguerras said, "is Dr. Sierra." He added significantly, "He is discreet."

Of Sierra Rennert never obtained more than a vague impression of a gloomy face, a pair of imposing waxed mustaches and a strong reek of brandy.

He led them into the chilly interior of the place and to the southeast corner. He directed his flashlight toward what lay on the boards.

Tresguerras' face did not lose any of its impassivity. "Quién es?"

Rennert told him.

Just for a moment there was a rather dangerous glint in the black eyes.

"I had not expected to find the dead man one of my countrymen." He stressed the Spanish sibilants. "The embassy of the United States told us something of this matter. As it seemed to be an affair of their citizens we agreed to let you take charge. We did not know there was danger to one of ours."

"Nor did I expect it," Rennert admitted. "Unfortunately this man was not altogether without blame. Come. While the doctor finishes I will tell you. These men will remove the body?"

Tresguerras walked with Rennert to the doorway. He listened, staring out into the night, to a succinct statement. He stepped aside as the two policemen went out with a plank upon which lay the flattened form of the murdered man. He bade the doctor good night. "Continue, Señor Rennert."

Rennert concluded, "That is the situation. It is difficult to know what to do. It is, primarily, the affair of the United States Embassy. My advice is to put the disposition of it into their hands."

The Mexican was silent for a moment. A Mexican's silence can be very expressive.

"Is there not danger," he said, "that the embassy will hush the matter and let the murderer go without punishment?"

"I will promise to see that the murderer is punished."

"Muy bien," Tresguerras agreed. "I have confidence in you, Señor Rennert."

"Gracias."

"You are certain that you are right about the identity?"

From the right-hand pocket of his vest Rennert produced two small sealed envelopes.

He gave them to the Mexican and said, "As certain as I can be until you give me a report on these."

"They are . . . ?"

"Bullets from two 32 caliber revolvers. One of them was taken from the skull of the first murdered man. I want them compared."

"Tonight?"

"There's no need of such haste. I can't interrupt the sleep or the amusement of the embassy at this hour. May I call in the morning?"

"Sí."

"At ten?"

"At ten."

A few minutes later Rennert was in his room removing his wet shoes and socks. As he put on slippers his face was stern and thoughtful, and the grim set of his lips made almost unrecognizable the tune which he was whistling.

It was that air from Gilbert and Sullivan which Dr. Drexel had whistled that hot afternoon in Laredo:

"*. . . Let the punishment fit the crime . . .*"

He suppressed a yawn of weariness, lit a cigarette and sat down at the secretary. He took the bundle of letters which had been the object of Professor Voice's study, slipped off the rubber band and began to turn them over with slow fingers.

He did not stop until the dimming of the light told him that the electric battery was nearing exhaustion.

As he undressed he philosophized sleepily upon how profoundly trivialities of one day—a woman's favorite recipe, a lover's message, a dinner invitation—could alter the course of life three quarters of a century later.

It wasn't until he was about to climb into bed that he remembered the door.

He walked over and turned the key in the lock. After all, the murderer was still free.

25
HAND

DELANEY ROARK LIVED in one of the larger and more pretentious apartment houses which have sprouted in the Colonia Roma, south of the United States Embassy and the Avenida Chapultepec.

Rennert, surveying its modernistic façade as he went up the sidewalk, found his conviction reinforced that the charm of Mexico City was being destroyed by foreign architectural importations. Comfortable, convenient, but . . .

He shrugged and passed by the sleepy gaze of the concierge into a carpeted hall full of imitation colonial chairs, potted tropical palms, American bridge lamps and Puebla urns. He located Roark's quarters and pressed the bell. He had to wait several moments before the door was opened.

Roark was in shirt sleeves and exuded a faint hygienic aroma of soap and shaving lotion. The toilet had not been able to remove the evidence of strain or dissipation, however. His eyes were dull and slightly bloodshot, and lines etched their corners. The skin of his face was sallow.

His frown vanished as he recognized his visitor. "Why, good morning, Mr. Rennert. Come in."

"It's an early hour for a call, but I wanted to talk to you before you went to the embassy."

"Perfectly all right."

Roark ushered him into a living room which was in considerable disarray. Ash trays were overflowing, newspapers lay scattered on the floor, and the gray felt hat, still damp, reposed where it had

been tossed upon a table. The air was stale and musty with over-
night smoke and pervasive whisky fumes.

"Had breakfast?" Roark asked as he raised a blind. His eyes
blinked as the morning sunshine poured in.

"Yes."

"I have coffee and rolls sent up every morning. I was just finishing my coffee. I'll bring it in if you don't mind."

He went out and returned in a moment, cup in hand. He found
Rennert ensconced in an overstuffed chair, administering to his
nose with a handkerchief.

"Catch cold last night?" he inquired.

"Yes. I got my feet wet digging."

"Digging?" in a tone of puzzlement.

"Yes. I got interested in the *tecolotes* which bothered Professor Voice and dug one up."

Roark sank onto the sofa and threw one leg over the other. "Oh,
that one we buried under the cedar tree?"

"Yes."

"I see." He gulped some of the coffee avidly. "Did the result justify
your cold?" he asked in an offhand manner as he set the cup down.

"Yes," Rennert said. "It did."

There was a moment of silence while the other took out a cigarette and searched in the smoke stand for a match. He found one,
lit it, and his eyes stared into its flame for a moment.

"Why don't you tell me what you've learned?" he suggested. "I
may be able to comprehend it now that I've had some coffee."

"That's why I'm here. I'm returning to Laredo today. I wanted
to see you unofficially before I went to the embassy."

The light, sharply defined eyebrows rose. "You don't mean
you're giving up the case?"

"I've done all that I can. I'm going to put the results into your
hands. When I've finished you can tell me what's to be done."

"All right. Go ahead." Roark's lips were occupied with the cigarette, and his eyes were narrowed against its smoke.

"First," Rennert began, his voice quiet, conversational, "the
extortion letters and the *tecolotes*. Weikel confessed to me last

night that he was responsible for both. As you know, he had felt resentment toward Voice for a long time on account of his failure to make Phi Beta Kappa. Last April the question of a job with the Teague Museum came up. Both Weikel and Biggerstaff put in applications, although it was fairly certain that Biggerstaff would get the place on account of his scholastic record. This renewed and intensified Weikel's grudge. He cast about for some way to vent his spite on the professor and hit upon the idea of the letters. In the drawings he made use, more or less consciously, of the clay figurines which were always before his eyes. The owls were merely an elaboration. The Pedregal, as we were told, abounds in them, but they seldom venture near the house. You remember Lucy Faudree telling about the mousetraps which Weikel set?"

"Yes."

"He used mice to draw the owls to Voice's window. He would hang them by a string just above the upper sash, where they couldn't be seen from the room. This attracted more and more *tecolotes* every night, of course. He saw to it that Voice knew of the superstition that their screeching foretold death. Thus he felt he was avenging his wrongs on the professor. A childish and sadistic procedure which tells a great deal about the young fellow's mental and emotional processes. But enough of that. The second thing I've learned is that Voice had in his possession the sum of twenty-five thousand pesos on the night of May first."

"How do you know that?" Roark was listening intently, his eyes shifting only momentarily from Rennert's face to the cigarette.

"You remember I found in the pocket of Voice's coat an envelope, on the back of which he had written a series of numbers. Their significance finally dawned on me. They were the numbers of lottery tickets which he had bought. The man was desperate for money with which to pay the supposed extortionist and resorted to this means of obtaining some. In one of the drawers of my wardrobe I found a newspaper dated May 2, with a list of the winning numbers in the National Lottery drawing of the previous day. One of Voice's numbers won twenty-five thousand pesos."

Rennert took the torn section of the paper from his pocket and passed it to Roark. The latter glanced at it without comment and started to hand it back. "There's a news item beside the lottery advertisement which you might read," Rennert said.

The other perused this, then laughed slightly as his fingers creased it. "Do you think that's apropos?"

"I should think so."

"I suppose so. Go ahead with your story."

"Someone knew about Voice's luck. Probably had seen the tickets which he had purchased and noted their numbers, foreseeing the possibility of taking advantage of the extortionist farce in case the man *did* obtain some money. At any rate, this person threw a stone through Voice's window that night, after the latter had got home from Mexico City. About the stone was a note, supposedly from the anonymous letter writer. Voice was reminded that now he had no excuse for not paying. The entire twenty-five thousand may have been demanded. Voice agreed to leave the money on the Pedregal that night. You agree that we have here a motive for his murder, don't you?"

Roark hesitated, his lower lip drawn in.

"Yes," he said slowly, "twenty-five thousand peso would certainly be a motive."

"I don't know exactly what happened that night," Rennert went on. "I think that Voice left the money on the lava, then hid to see who would carry it off. When he did see who it was, he confronted this person. The shooting of Voice was probably an impulsive action, regretted as soon as it was done. The disposition of the body was simple, with digging implements and lime in the coach house. It took but a few minutes to undress Voice and bury him by the wall. The clothing, of course, would be burned to avoid identification. Unfortunately for the murderer, a Phi Beta Kappa key fell from his watch chain while he was digging."

Roark leaned forward, his nostrils flaring. "A Phi Beta Kappa key!" he echoed,

"Yes, the murderer is a Phi Beta Kappa. Membership in that fraternity can be proven easily enough, of course. That key, bearing his name, remained with the body of his victim until last week. The murderer may have been unaware that he had dropped it in such a compromising place. He may have decided that it would be too risky to disinter the body, so trusted that it would never be found. But he hadn't counted on the heavy rains at the beginning of the summer. They washed a gully along that wall and exposed Voice's skeleton and the key. Now, as to how that skeleton came to be in the shipment which we found at the border. I have here a statement from Dr. Fogarty. It's self-explanatory.' "

Roark read this through, slowly at first, then more hurriedly.

"I see," he said as he returned it. "That explains the conversation between Fogarty and Echave which you overheard."

"Yes. Echave intended to abstract one of the prehistoric skeletons and sell it to a private collector. But when Marta showed him the skeleton which the rains had exposed it doubtless appealed to his sense of humor to put this in the plaster cast in place of the other. A characteristic Mexican touch. I feel sure that he didn't know it was the body of a murdered man. He probably didn't examine it closely. If he had known or even suspected what it really was, I'm sure he wouldn't have taken the risk. He had nothing to gain by it, since the difference in age of the bones would be detected at the museum. Later he found this Phi Beta Kappa key in the same spot. He thought it was a gold coin and suspended it about his neck.

"That's my reconstruction of everything that happened up to my arrival on the scene. I'm satisfied that in the main it's correct. Then the murderer learned that two things threatened his safety: the letter which he had sent to Lucy Faudree with Voice's signature and which Monica had kept; the key with his name on it, which was on Echave's person. He made two attempts to secure the letter. One, while Monica was out of the room before dinner; the other, while she was downstairs eating. The second time she returned sooner than he had expected. As nearly as I can gather from her account this morning, he hid in the wardrobe when he heard her coming, then, when she went to the bath, secured the letter and got away. It's evident, then, that the murderer was in possession of or could be identified with the typewriter on which that letter was written. There remained the Phi Beta Kappa key. He made an engagement with Echave to meet him in the coach house. He killed him with a pick and hid the body, intending to return later and bury it as he had that of his first victim. Have I stated everything clearly? Any questions or comments?"

Roark's brows were drawn together in a frown.

"No," he said. "You've stated it very well, Rennert. But I can't see that you have any proof of the murderer's identity. The type-written letter has doubtless been destroyed by now. So that's out. You don't have the Phi Beta Kappa key. Its owner may have hidden it or may even be wearing it. In either case you can't prove that it's the one Echave found."

"Aren't you forgetting the proof which I *do* have? Two bullets, both from the same 37 caliber revolver. One of them found in Voice's skull."

Roark leaned back and tapped a fingernail against his front teeth as he stared fixedly at a picture on the opposite wall. "Have you had these bullets compared yet?"

"Lieutenant Tresguerras brought them to Mexico City last night. I am to get the report of the ballistics expert this morning."

"So you had to bring the police into it?"

"It was unavoidable after Echave's murder. They've given me permission to terminate the case as I see fit, however."

"When are you going to get the report on those bullets?"

"At ten."

"Then I suppose you'll see the old man?"

"Yes. Do you want to go with me?"

Roark lit another cigarette. He held it between his lips for a long time without seeming to draw upon it. He removed it finally and spat away a shred of tobacco. "No. I'd rather not. Did I under-stand correctly—that I can say what is to be done before things go any farther?"

"Yes."

Roark looked at him. "Do you mind telling me why, Rennert?"

"For one reason, because both of us will wish as little scandal as possible stirred up. Then, too, my personal feelings enter into this a bit. I have been involved, more or less against my will, in several murder cases. This is the first one in which I have understood the extenuating circumstances so well. I'm not a professional detective or a policeman, thank God. I can put my own interpretation on justice. I think you'll understand how I feel."

"I do." Roark got up abruptly, threw back his shoulders and took a deep breath. "May I think it over a few minutes?"

"Yes. I shall not make any report at the embassy until ten. Shall I call you then?"

"Yes, if you will."

Rennert was on his feet, pulling down his coat. "I scarcely feel presentable enough to show myself at the embassy. I came away from the Faudree house wearing a gun in this holster." He touched his left side. "I'm afraid its bulge is too conspicuous. What do you think?"

"I agree with you."

"May I leave it here?"

"All right."

Rennert removed the revolver and laid it on a table.

Roark's eyes fastened on it. "That's not Cornell's, is it?"

"No. This is my own."

Roark hesitated. "Have you seen Cornell?"

"Not this morning."

"When you do, tell her that I'm sorry all this had to happen at her house, will you?"

"Certainly. Anything else?"

"That's all. Well, Mr. Rennert, adiós."

"Adiós, Roark."

Their hands met.

At the touch of the older man's fingers, Roark's face stiffened. His eyes searched the light-brown ones for an instant. Then he laughed so uncontrollably that his shoulders shook and his voice was unsteady.

"You keep your surprises well, Rennert."

26
HAT

ON THE LAWN OUTSIDE a window of the United States Embassy a
mower sliced blades of grass still wet from the night's rain. The
bougainvillaea looked splattered with fresh paint, intensely bright.

The man who sat at a desk by this window was looking at neither
the bougainvillaea nor the grass nor the spun silk of the Mexican sky,
however. He was probably unaware of the metallic clatter of the lawn
mower. He was gazing across the mahogany surface and saying:

"You work fast, Mr. Rennert."

Rennert was drawing dubiously upon a cigar. It was a little too
soon after breakfast to be consuming such a large and black cigar,
however excellent the quality. He said:

"Things moved fast. I only tried to keep up with them."

"You seem to have been successful." A clearing of the throat.
"But now we come to the crux of the question—the identity of the
murderer. You haven't told me that yet." (Rennert's recital so far
had been almost identical with that in Roark's apartment.)

Rennert glanced at his watch. "May I use your telephone?"

"Why certainly."

Rennert called the office of Lieutenant Tresguerras. After greet-
ings had been exchanged he asked, "Did your ballistics expert compare the markings on those two bullets?" There was an answer.
Rennert said, "Thank you. I was sure they would," and hung up.

He looked across the desk. "You stated in this office yesterday
that I might name my compensation for my efforts in this case. Is
that correct?"

"Why—certainly. That will be arranged. Anything you say. Within reason, of course."

"What I want is your sanction for something I have already done. You will understand in a moment."

Rennert took up the telephone again. "The apartment of Delaney Roark," he said to the switchboard operator.

The man at the desk heard:

"Rennert speaking, Roark. I'm at the embassy. I have called police headquarters. The two bullets match. . . . Not yet. . . . I thought you would. Yes, I'll hold it."

Rennert took the receiver from his ear and held it away a few inches as he waited.

The sound of the shot carried across the smooth mahogany of the desk.

Rennert let the receiver fall and stared at crimson and magenta bougainvillaea.

It was several seconds before the other man spoke: "Rennert, do you mean . . . ?"

The cigar had been a mistake. Rennert compressed his lips as he ground it into a tray.

"Of course," he said gruffly. "The murderer was Delaney Roark. The bullet in Voice's skull matched the bullet from his gun which I found in the body of an owl he killed six weeks ago."

The swivel chair creaked as a heavy body shifted backwards. Again there was a long silence, during which the two men did not look at each other. The lawn mower whirred on,

"Do you want to tell me now, Mr. Rennert?"

Rennert sat down. His normally soft, rather slow voice was hurried and clipped:

"A hat was the first thing that made me consider Roark as suspect. He was bareheaded when he and I went to the coach house yesterday afternoon. He left me there, looking through Voice's belongings, while he went to the plaza with the chauffeur. When he returned, some time later, he was wearing a hat, the same hat which I knew he had put on a rack in the hall. Yet he told me that he had left my gladstone in the car because he had no key to the house. It was a little thing, but it made me wonder. All the more so when I learned that during the time he was gone someone had entered Monica Faudree's room and searched for the letter which had arrived after Voice's death. If he had gone into the house, I thought, he had taken his hat to justify his presence there, should anyone see him, then had neglected to replace it. Later, while he was supposed to be in Mexico City, the same room was entered again. This time the letter was stolen. That letter, then, was essential to someone's security. Yet as far as I was aware, only Roark and I knew that Monica had it. Why, I asked myself, was it so incriminating? There were two typewriters in the house, Voice's own and Dr. Fogarty's. If it were proven that the typing was that of either of those machines, no one individual would be seriously implicated. Fogarty's machine was borrowed frequently by his assistants. I remembered then that I was carrying in my pocket the letter of credentials which you had Roark write out for me on his machine here in the embassy. There, I saw, was an explanation. Roark had typed the supposed letter from Voice on the same machine. Had I obtained that letter I would have had in my pocket all the evidence required. At any moment I might be prompted to make a comparison of the typing."

Rennert heard a murmur which mingled with that of the lawn mower. It sounded like, "My God, right here in the embassy!"

He went on: "I saw how Roark could enter the house so readily without announcing his presence by knocking. It was possible that he had kept a key which he had found in Voice's pocket, but I doubted that. I remembered that he had helped me undress young Biggerstaff. When I searched Biggerstaff's clothing I didn't find the key with which he had unlocked the front door upon our arrival. While Roark was not the only person who might have taken that key, he at least had had the opportunity. But I could think of no possible motive which he might have had for killing Voice until I learned of the lottery ticket. I knew the kind of life a young bachelor in the diplomatic service would be leading, even before Cornell Faudree told me of his debts. I knew that the salary which he was receiving here couldn't be a large one. It was reasonable to assume that twenty-five thousand pesos would have tempted him, particularly since he would think that Voice would leave it on the Pedregal for someone else if he didn't take it. Voice had a key to the upstairs storeroom of the coach house, so from there Roark had access through a trap door in the loft to the room where the shovels and lime of the archaeological party were kept."

"But this Mexican inspector—Echave—you mean that Delaney murdered him too? So brutally, with that pick?"

"Yes. He was beside himself with fear lest he be found out. I admit that for a moment there I considered Dr. Fogarty in the role of murderer. The removal of Echave coincided so nicely with the implication of the Mexican in the theft of the archaeological specimens and his suggestion of a possible motive for the latter's murder of Voice. Had I not found Echave's body when I did it would have been buried. The supposition would have been that he had fled because of his guilt. But the embassy chauffeur, when he returned from shadowing Echave, told me that Roark had spoken to Echave on the plaza before the latter boarded the Mexico City streetcar. Also, that Roark's orders had been that it was not necessary to follow Echave back to San Angel. I saw what Roark had done. Under the pretense of identifying Echave for the chauffeur's benefit, he had made an appointment with the inspector to meet him at the coach house before the time for his appointment with Fogarty. Then he saw to it that the chauffeur was not present when Echave returned. He killed him in order to obtain the Phi Beta Kappa key which he had dropped in Voice's grave."

"But how did you know that Delaney was a Phi Beta Kappa?"

"I didn't, but I remembered your saying that he had an excellent college record in the United States. I thought it likely that this would have carried Phi Beta Kappa membership. This morning I shook hands with him and gave him the fraternity grip. He returned it automatically."

The swivel chair creaked very faintly. "I see. You—went to his apartment?"

"Yes. I let him know that I was convinced of his guilt. I gave him a newspaper clipping which contained the numbers that had won prizes in the lottery. In the next column was a news item about a suicide who had staked all his money on the drawing but hadn't won. I gave my gun to Roark."

Rennert got up. "Over the phone just now he told me that my reconstruction of his actions was correct. I trust, then, that my report is satisfactory. I'm leaving for the border this afternoon."

The man at the desk seemed to have recovered from his agitation of a few minutes before. His eyes had a speculative look, as if his thoughts had journeyed on to something else. His fingertips were joined and tapping lightly on his chin.

"Yes, yes," he murmured. "Quite satisfactory. There will be a certain amount of scandal, of course. That's unavoidable. But I think it can be hushed up soon. It need have no repercussions on my— But tell me, Mr. Rennert, how did you happen to know the Phi Beta Kappa grip? I thought those things were supposed to be kept a secret?"

Rennert said dryly, "I went to college once myself."

27
END

Dear Mr. Rennert:

I thought I would write you a letter rather than send you a Christmas card. I was going to write several times this fall, but I have been very busy here at the museum.

I am sending you a clipping from a Mexico City newspaper about the auction sale of the postage stamps on those old letters of Lucy's. It says that the most valuable of them were Postmaster issues. I did not know what that meant, but I looked it up and it means stamps that the postmasters in the South made themselves before the Confederacy issued regular stamps. I had no idea that anybody would pay so much for old stamps until you told us last summer. It was certainly lucky for Cornell and me that you thought of that.

Cornell is well and sends her best wishes. We are very happy and have rented a small house. I wish you could see it. It is very nice and comfortable.

We had a letter from Monica last week, and she says that she is coming up on a visit next month. She says she is going to stay several months, as she thinks Cornell will need her. We are very glad to have her come to visit us, but I do not really think it is necessary.

You may see Monica, since she is coming through Laredo, and writes that she is bringing some baby clothes that she and Lucy

180

made, and she wants to know if she will have to pay duty on them. She says she hopes you can arrange it, because she does not think there ought to be a duty on such things. I do not know.

Well, I must close as it is getting late.

Very sincerely yours,
John Clay Biggers

The Cat Screams
ISBN 1-61646-148-9

VULTURES
IN THE SKY
A HUGH RENNERT MYSTERY

TODD DOWNING

Vultures in the Sky
ISBN 1-61646-149-7

Murder on the Tropic
ISBN 1-61646-150-0

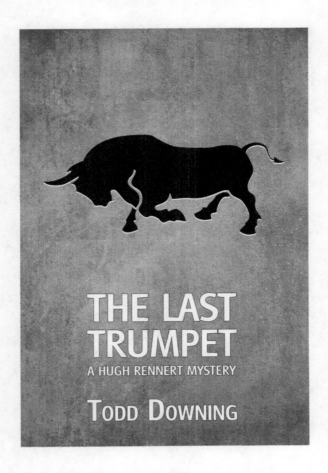

The Last Trumpet
ISBN 1-61646-152-7

Night Over Mexico
ISBN 1-61646-153-5

CLUES AND CORPSES
The Detective Fiction and
Mystery Criticism of Todd Downing
CURTIS EVANS

Clues and Corpses: The Detective Fiction and
Mystery Criticism of Todd Downing
Curtis Evans
ISBN 1-61646-145-4

www.ingramcontent.com/pod-product-compliance
Lightning Source LLC
LaVergne TN
LVHW022341300125
802637LV00006B/317